CODEBUSTERS

Bloomsbury Education
An imprint of Bloomsbury Publishing Plc

50 Bedford Square
London
WC1B 3DP
UK

1385 Broadway
New York
NY 10018
USA

www.bloomsbury.com

First published in Great Britain 2017
This paperback edition published in 2017

ISBN PB: 978 1 4729 4341 5
ePub: 978 1 4729 4339 2
ePDF: 978 1 4729 4342 2

2 4 6 8 10 9 7 5 3 1

Typeset by Newgen Knowledge Works (P) Ltd., Chennai, India
Printed and bound by CPI Group (UK) Ltd, Croydon CD0 4YY

To find out more about our authors and books visit www.bloomsbury.com.
Here you will find extracts, author interviews, details of forthcoming events and
the option to sign up for our newsletters.

CODEBUSTERS

DAN METCALF

illustrated by **GARY CHERRINGTON**

BLOOMSBURY EDUCATION
AN IMPRINT OF BLOOMSBURY
LONDON OXFORD NEW YORK NEW DELHI SYDNEY

To Sheba x

Contents

Chapter One

The thing about parents is they haven't got a clue.

They don't know how hard it is being the new kid in school, especially coming in halfway through a term. They don't know how hard it is to be cool, to be seen as the mysterious guy with the ace trainers and a mean overhead kick on the pitch. They don't know how hard it is to fit in.

I moved to Bletchley Grange School halfway through the autumn term 'cos of Mum's stupid job. She moved us away from the city and into the boring brick suburbs, and away from my old school. Bletchley seemed all right, but coming in late meant that everyone had already found their mates. I have a theory: the first two weeks of secondary school will decide your entire life. You'll choose who your mates are, what subjects

7

you'll be good at and, most importantly, you'll be labelled for life. Take my uncle Nick for example. When he arrived at school on the first day of term he had just got over chickenpox, so everyone called him Spotty, and the name stuck. Twenty years later, he's still known as Spotty. He once said he wanted to be the town mayor, but he had no chance with a name like that.

Anyway, I made the same sort of mistake at my last school back in the city. I let on that I was good at maths, and that was it – I was nerdy Jackson Hilbert for my entire time there. In my old school I had already been labelled as a loser but now I have a chance, a fresh start, to become a new *cool* me – I'm not going to be nerdy Jackson any more. I'm *Jax* – and this time I'm not going to muck it up.

The school had old buildings but loads of brand-new equipment. Each room had a plasma screen and halfway through registration it flickered on and the head teacher's face appeared on it. Mr Kirrin was about fifty, but he looked older. His hair had turned grey to match his suit, probably due to stress and lack of sleep.

'Good morning, Bletchley Grange. I have a few things to bring to your attention. Firstly, the upper corridor in C Block is out of bounds for the time being after a student saw fit to consume ten bags of sweets for a bet and was promptly sick down the entire length of the building.'

All eyes in my class turned to a stocky kid sitting at the back of the room.

'What?' he shrugged. 'I still won the bet!'

'And I'm pleased to tell you that Jasper Newton and Michelle Chang have won our first major trophy of the year by finishing first in the regional mathematics championship. Please join me in congratulating them on their success.'

Mr Kirrin clapped enthusiastically, while the entire class stayed completely still, not even attempting to show any support for the trophy winners. Instead they looked glumly at the screen, a few rolling their eyeballs in boredom.

'And lastly,' continued Mr Kirrin, 'I am happy to announce that later this week the new eco-boiler underneath Q Block will be activated for the first time. I would remind students that all rubbish should be put into the correct bins so that the new eco-boiler can burn the suitable waste to provide us with energy and heat. That is all.'

I looked back down at my desk.

'Oh, and one last thing,' said Mr Kirrin, 'could you please give a special Bletchley welcome to Jackson Hilbert, who has just joined us. Hmm, Jackson, what a peculiar name. Welcome aboard!'

I sank down in my seat while the eyes of my class turned to me.

'Jackson? Why are you called Jackson?' said one girl.

'My, er, mum. She really liked Michael Jackson,' I explained.

'So...' said vomit-boy in the back row. 'Why didn't she just call you Michael?'

I sighed.

'I ask myself that every day.'

My form teacher handed me my timetable, a map of the school, and told me to follow the rest of the kids to the first lesson. No one introduced themselves, but I hadn't expected them to. I knew that I would have to make a big impression to be popular, so I had a plan. In my old school I had noticed that the popular kids were never that good in class, but they were always great at football. I'd been rubbish at sports, which was why I'd never been popular. So in my head it was a simple sum: Good at football equals popular; Jax wants to be popular, *therefore* Jax needs to be good at football. I already knew I couldn't kick a ball straight to save my life, but I *could* be good in goal. All I had to do was get into a kickabout at lunchtime, then I'd be set. Cool Jax, on my way.

But first: double maths.

I found my way to the classroom easily and I managed to sit in the perfect non-nerd position: halfway back, on the side, next to a window. Any closer would look too eager, any further back I would look like a slacker and attract too much attention. The teacher, Miss Almond, said hello and did the register. She was nice. I even managed to get her to call me Jax.

I knew that if I let on I was good at maths I'd be cruelly mocked and my plan to be the coolest kid in town would be ruined. So when Miss Almond asked me where we'd got to in my old school, I just fibbed and made out that I hadn't done much. I planned to keep quiet and keep my work as average as possible. We started off with some basic algebra. I knew how to do it, but made a show of biting my pen and scratching my head in concentration.

Twenty minutes into the lesson, Miss Almond had put up a problem on the board.

'Can anyone tell me the value of z in this sum?'

The class stared at her, no one raising their hands.

'Come on, we did this last week,' she pleaded.

Still no one. I knew the answer, but I would look like a total loser if I piped up now. At that moment the classroom door opened and I looked up. A girl walked in, pretty and Asian-looking, wearing a simple blouse and skirt. She closed the door quietly.

'Sorry I'm late, miss,' she said, her voice strong with confidence. 'Dentist.'

'That's fine, Michelle,' said Miss Almond. 'Take a seat and help me out with the problem on the board, please.'

'Sixteen,' said Michelle, before she'd even reached her desk. She must have worked it out in the seconds she had been inside the room. I was a bit shocked by how confidently she had said the answer, not apologetically like I would have done, like I was risking ridicule from the rest of the class for being a boffin.

'Excellent! So if we change this number, what does z become? Jax?'

'Twenty-four, miss,' I said without even thinking.

'Well done! And so quick!'

Oh no. I had got it right. I'd been so distracted by Michelle that I'd forgotten to be clueless at maths. I had barely heard the question and I had just blurted out the correct answer.

'Looks like we might have a contender for maths champion, Michelle. You had better watch your back!'

I had to undo this.

'I don't think so, miss,' I said. 'It was just a lucky guess.'

'Yes, miss. Probably a fluke,' said Michelle.

Hang on. Why did she think that? She'd been in the room for less than a minute and she thought she could judge me well enough to know it was a fluke!

'Ask me another, then,' I said.

What? No! Shut up, Jackson! I mean, Jax.

'Oh, okay,' said Miss Almond. 'If I change this number, what does y become?'

'Thirty-six.'

Correct again. What was I doing? The problem was I could never back down from a challenge and Michelle seemed to have pushed all the right buttons into getting me to expose myself as a maths whizz.

'Interesting,' said Miss Almond. 'Looks like we might have a maths battle on our hands!'

'I doubt it, miss,' said Michelle. 'You can't tell after just a couple of sums.'

WHAT? By now, all thoughts of trying to look like Mr Average were gone and I wanted to defend my honour as a maths nerd.

'Jax, do you know what a prime number is?' asked Miss Almond.

'Yes, miss,' I answered. 'It's a number that can only be divided by one and itself.'

'Excellent. Let's have a bit of fun, shall we?' she said.

Miss Almond explained the game. Michelle and I had to stand up, and we'd take turns saying prime numbers, starting from two. The first to get one wrong or hesitate was out. It was like a sudden-death penalty shoot-out for geeks.

I stood up and saw the whole class looking at me. I didn't care any more. I had already revealed myself to be a nerd. I might as well be the *biggest* nerd.

'Two,' I started.

'Three,' said Michelle.

'Five.'

'Seven.'

'Eleven.'

'Thirteen.'

We were shouting out the numbers thick and fast and Miss Almond was encouraging the class to cheer and support us. I noticed that all the boys seemed to be egging me on, while all the girls were behind Michelle. This was – in its own weird way – kind of cool. We carried on with the prime numbers and it was testing my knowledge. I only really knew up to the fiftieth prime number, so I prayed Michelle knew less than me.

'Fifty-three.'

'Fifty-nine.'

'Sixty-one.'

'Sixty-seven.'

This was getting heated, like a world cup final. Michelle seemed to be into it too. Her title as maths queen was under threat. You could see this really mattered to her.

'A hundred and one.'

'A hundred and three.'

'A hundred and seven.'

'A hundred and nine.'

This was tricky now. I was searching my head for the next one and it looked like Michelle was getting tired too.

'A hundred and fifty-one,' I shouted.

'A hundred and fifty-seven,' said Michelle smugly.

'A hundred and sixty-three?' I chanced.

'A hundred and sixty-seven,' said Michelle.

She was grinning now, knowing I was close to desperately guessing random numbers.

'A hundred and eighty-one?' I asked. Miss Almond nodded.

'A hundred and eighty-seven!' shouted Michelle.

I stopped.

'What's the matter? Run out of steam?' said Michelle, smiling.

'It's not a prime.'

'What?' said Michelle, crestfallen.

'A hundred and eighty-seven is not a prime number,' I said. I hoped I was right. If I wasn't, I would have forfeited the game.

'Oh! Yes! Quite true! It's divisible by eleven and seventeen!' said Miss Almond, who was amazingly excited. 'Jax is the winner!'

The boys gave a half-hearted cheer and the class turned around to face the board again. Michelle and I were left standing. She looked so sad, like I'd robbed her of her crown – which I had, I suppose. I consoled myself with the thought that I may have found a friend, if she forgave me, in the one person who was at least as good at maths as me.

The rest of the lesson continued quietly and I didn't raise my hand to offer any more answers. Neither did Michelle. I looked back at her a few times and she looked crushed, her eyes fixed on the work in front of her.

At the end of the lesson, I gathered my things and looked at my timetable.

'Can you tell me where the music classroom is?' I asked one boy. He laughed at me.

'You're the genius – you work it out!' he said. He and a bunch of other boys did the well-recognised sign for 'loser', pressing their thumb and forefinger up against their forehead in an 'L' shape.

'What a spanner!' said one boy.

'Nah, he's not even that – he's just a zero!' They all laughed.

'ZE-RO! ZE-RO! ZE-RO!' they chanted. Eventually they walked off, shouting out random numbers in a robot voice.

'*Se-ven-teen! Twen-ty-three!*'

I saw Michelle turning to leave too. I rushed over to her.

'Hey, Michelle! Good game earlier. No hard feelings, yeah?'

She looked up and glared at me. It was clear there were *plenty* of hard feelings.

'Excuse me,' she muttered, and barged past me, knocking me into a desk.

Excellent. In the course of one morning, I had managed to prove myself to be the biggest nerd in the year, got myself the lamest nickname ever and upset the only other person who might have been my friend.

Luckily I managed to get through the rest of the day without any more major embarrassments. There was a slight incident at lunch where I almost choked on a crisp, then coughed so hard that chocolate milk came out of my nose, but I'm not sure anyone noticed. Except the girl who I sprayed milk over.

I went out of the school gates and set off home. The walk should take about twenty minutes, but I'd seen a path through a park next to the school that could cut some time off my journey. I was desperate to get back and try to forget about the day, so I entered the park. I'd seen loads of kids walk past the gates, taking the long way round, and I hadn't thought to wonder why.

'Empty your bag, loser.'

That was why. Three beefy skinhead boys in hoodies were blocking the path, the light of the autumn sun glinting off their heads. I sighed, and handed over my bag.

'You're new,' said the biggest one. I nodded. 'Most kids know not to come through here. This is *our* park.'

'I'll try to remember that,' I said. They were older than me and they all looked the same – shaved heads, stocky frames. They all had furrowed eyebrows, which made them look as though they were constantly angry. They rifled through my bag, taking some leftover sandwiches and half a bottle of lemonade.

'We're the Bragg brothers,' said the youngest. 'I'm Dan, this is Dave, and that's Dom.'

'Pleased to meet you,' I lied. For bullies, they were very chatty.

'What's your name?' he demanded.

'Jackson – I mean, Jax.'

Dom (or was it Dave? I'd lost track already) was still going through my bag. He lifted out a pair of goalkeeper's gloves. I'd stashed them there as part of my cool-new-Jax plan. If anyone had asked me to play, I'd have been ready, but after my nerd demonstration no one had asked and now I guessed I'd be lucky if they let me play as the goal*post*, never mind the goal*keeper*.

'You play in goal?' the biggest Bragg said. I nodded. 'You any good?'

'Um... yeah. I do all right.'

'Nice. Come back here tomorrow after school, we can have a kickabout.'

'Really?' I smiled. 'Great! Does that mean you're going to stop mugging me?'

The three brothers laughed like I had just told them my best joke about a jellyfish and the Queen's knickers.

'No. Turn out your pockets.'

I reached into my pockets and felt around. I pulled out about £3.57 in change and a used tissue. In my other pocket were my keys, a small plastic toy soldier and a business card that definitely hadn't been there before. The Braggs took my money and told me to get lost, making me promise to come back the next day for a friendly kickabout. (*Friendly?*)

I got home and found Mum was home early from work, doing an exercise DVD in the lounge.

'Hiya, love! How was your first day?' she said, breathless and sweaty.

Disastrous. Horrible. Complete nightmare.

'All right,' I said. Well, she wouldn't understand. She doesn't have to worry about being cool. She jumped on the spot and started doing a belly-dance hip shimmy to the DVD.

'Did you make any friends?' she puffed.

Hmm. I made an enemy of someone I could have got on really well with and a friend of three boys that may still beat me up.

'Sort of. Not really.'

'Ah well,' she said breathlessly. 'Might take a while. Go get yourself sorted, I've got fajitas in the oven.'

I went to my room and changed. I emptied out my pockets and saw the business card again. Where had that come from? I put it on my desk and turned the lamp on to take a closer look. On it was a random collection of letters written in pen, signed at the bottom with a symbol.

LHM ICEJ HPR 8PJ

張

Chapter Two

After a few moments of confusion, I suddenly realised what I was looking at.

A code.

Someone had written a code on a card and slipped it into my pocket, like a spy in one of Grandad's old books. Whenever we had gone to stay with Grandad, I'd always get down one of his dusty old books and leaf through it absently. The books looked dense and dull, but Grandad would explain what each one was about, and he'd come alive as he told me stories about spies, soldiers, bombs and evil geniuses that wanted to destroy the world. He had grown up during the Second World War and had collected loads of fantastic adventures and stories about it. When he passed away he left me all his books, which were still in boxes from our move.

Mum called me for dinner and I went downstairs. We ate our fajita and chips in front of the telly.

'Mum, did you ever read any of Grandad's old war books?'

'Some. He probably re-enacted the rest of them for me. Why?'

'What were codes used for?'

Mum chewed on a chip as she thought.

'Codes? They were used to pass messages from one person to another. If the enemy got hold of the message, they wouldn't be able to understand it.'

'What if the message was passed to someone who didn't know the code?' I asked.

'Then it could have been a test, or an initiation. If you managed to work out the code, then you'd prove you were smart enough to join the team. Is this homework?'

'Yeah, I suppose it is.'

When we had finished eating, I gathered up the plates and took them through to the kitchen. I plonked them in the sink and turned round, where Mum was waiting with a smile on her face.

'Surprise!' she chimed, holding out her hands. In them was a small wrapped package.

'What's this?'

'Call it a well-done-on-surviving-your-first-day-at-school present. And a sorry-for-moving-us-halfway-across-the-country present.'

'Aw, Mum! You didn't need to do that.' I was glad she had though. I didn't tell her I very nearly *hadn't* survived the day. I unwrapped the present to find a snazzy smartphone.

'Don't get too excited. Work gave me a new phone, so I thought you could have my old one. You can keep in touch with me, text your mates and it'll stop you nicking my phone to play games on.'

This was actually really cool. Mum's old phone was only a few months old, and had loads of great features.

'Thanks, Mum!' I hugged her. 'Has it got –'

'All the latest games? Yes. You're welcome.'

I washed up and disappeared upstairs to the spare room, where I ripped open the box of Grandad's books. I was eager to play on my new phone, but just as keen to work out the mysterious code I had found. I searched though each book, hunting for clues as to what kind of code it was and how to crack it. A couple of hours later, I found the likeliest solution: it needed a keyword. To decipher it you first need a grid with the plain text, which is the normal alphabet:

CODE:													
TEXT:	A	B	C	D	E	F	G	H	I	J	K	L	M
CODE:													
TEXT:	N	O	P	Q	R	S	T	U	V	W	X	Y	Z

Underneath it in the first few boxes you place the keyword, followed by the rest of the alphabet in its usual letter order. From this, you can decode any message. The trouble is, you need to know the keyword and what one do you start with? It could be anything, which is the beauty of the system if you don't want someone to see your message, but when you're trying to crack it like I was, it's a little tricky...

Mum forced me to go to bed after I had spent even more time getting nowhere. As I lay in bed, nodding off to sleep, I held the business card in my hand. My tired brain was going over and over the code, inching closer to the solution that seemed so far away...

Chapter Three

I woke with a start the next morning and knew exactly what I needed to do. My brain had been filtering the code all night, searching for that missing keyword, my dreams decoding the message (apart from the one where I got chased around a double-decker bus by a monkey on stilts – that was just plain *weird*). And as soon as my eyes popped open, I had the answer.

I dressed in a hurry and rushed out of the door with a slice of toast in my hand. I told Mum I was going in early to do homework in the library. I walked to school, avoiding the park this time, going over the code in my head to be sure I was right. I definitely was, but what I hadn't figured out was why a certain someone had given the code to me.

I wandered through the school, consulting my map, until I found the rendezvous (I had learnt that word from Grandad's books too. It meant meeting place). Finally I walked down a dusty old corridor and came to a door with a sign on it that said 'Classroom out of use – do not enter'. I took a deep breath and entered.

The room was dark and smelt funny, like the windows hadn't been opened in years. There were rows of wooden benches with stools stacked on top, and posters of the periodic table on the walls. I was in the right place, but where was the other person?

'You're late,' said a voice from the back of the room. It made me jump, but I kept my cool.

'Not by my watch,' I said. It was gloomy and I couldn't make out a face, just a silhouette against a back window where the morning light was trying to filter through the dirty glass.

'You cracked the code,' said the voice.

'Obviously,' I said, sounding a bit too smug. 'Simple once you have the keyword.'

'Which is?'

They should know, I thought. They set it. They obviously wanted to check I hadn't stumbled upon it by accident, which was fine by me, as I was in the mood to show off.

'I knew I was looking for a small, significant word. The main clue was on the card. A Chinese symbol,' I said, strolling along the lines of benches towards the back of the room. 'There was only one person I knew who could have written that.'

I turned a corner and saw the person I had expected to meet.

'Me,' said Michelle the maths queen, with a slight smile. I smiled back.

'Exactly. You dropped the card into my pocket when you barged past me. Nice work! I don't know what the symbol means though.'

'Chang. My family name.'

'Of course! Well, once I knew who the note was from, working out the keyword was easy. There was only one word that could link us both: prime.'

I strolled up to her as coolly as I could (until I stumbled on my shoelace) and showed her the scrap of paper with my working on it:

CODE:	P	R	I	M	E	A	B	C	D	F	G	H	J
TEXT:	A	B	C	D	E	F	G	H	I	J	K	L	M
CODE:	K	L	N	O	Q	S	T	U	V	W	X	Y	Z
TEXT:	N	O	P	Q	R	S	T	U	V	W	X	Y	Z

'Bravo,' said Michelle. She was amazingly confident and kept a cool smirk on her lips the whole time.

'So what did you want to see me about?' I asked.

'She didn't,' said another voice from the back of the room. 'I did.'

I peered past Michelle into the gloom to the source of the voice. On a bench at the back of the class sat a dark-skinned boy, about the same age as me. He struck a match and lit a Bunsen burner with a flourish, illuminating a thin face with large, thick glasses, secured at the side with a bit of sticky tape. He wore a blazer and tie, which was odd, because Bletchley Grange doesn't have a uniform, and he had a giant afro.

'Welcome, Mr Hilbert,' said the boy.

'Who are you?' I asked. I had only expected to meet Michelle, and now there was some oddball at the back of the room with a box of matches and goodness knows what else.

'My name is Jasper Newton, but I'd appreciate it if you kept that top secret.'

'What's going on?'

'I would have thought that was obvious,' he said with a wonky grin that was clearly meant to be mysterious. 'You've been recruited.'

Whoever this guy was, he liked talking in riddles and keeping me guessing. He also had a talent for being dramatic, with the weird lighting and secret meetings. I hated to play along and be the idiot asking the questions, but he left me no choice.

'Recruited to what?'

'We, Mr Hilbert, are –' he paused for effect – 'The Codebusters!'

A pause. Jasper let the name hang in the air, the sound of his own voice echoing in the empty classroom. I think he expected a clap of thunder and lightning to light up the room, like he was in a bad 1960s horror movie. Just then, the door opened behind me and I heard another voice.

'Blimey, bit gloomy in here, ain't it?'

The fluorescent strip lights above us burst into life with a hum.

'That's better. What are you lot doing, sitting about in the dark?'

A large boy my own age with a mop of floppy blond hair stood in the doorway, a bag of crisps in his hand.

'I was attempting to add an air of mystery to the proceedings, but once again you've stomped all over that with your size fives,' said Jasper, sulkily extinguishing his Bunsen burner. The blond boy laughed a loud, warm laugh and dumped his school bag on the floor.

'Don't mind him, mate, he likes a bit of drama. You must be Jax,' he said, wiping his hand on his jeans and offering it to me to shake. 'Pleased to meet you. I'm –'

'I'll do the introductions, thank you!' interrupted Jasper.

'Suit yourself.'

Jasper rose and walked across to us. He was small, with patches on his trousers and untidy scuffed boots on his feet.

'I'm Jasper, the commander of the group. You could think of me as your sergeant major. You've already met Michelle Chang, my second-in-command. Her strength is word clues and mathematics. And this is Charlie Babbage, our spatial and physical expert.'

Charlie shook my hand finally.

'I just like puzzles.' He shrugged. I liked him immediately. He didn't seem to mess about like the other two.

'And so,' I said, not sure if I'd like the answer, 'what exactly *is* the Codebusters?'

Jasper perked up and began to stroll around the classroom like a peacock.

'Here he goes. Get comfy,' said Charlie, sitting on a bench and munching his bag of crisps.

'There is no mystery in life, Mr Hilbert,' said Jasper, 'which cannot be solved with science, reason and mathematics. The Codebusters exist to solve these puzzles by using our combined skills to thwart the enemy and bring the world to justice.'

He must have practised that speech. A lot.

'So... you're a crime-fighting gang?' I asked. Michelle laughed.

'You make us sound like a bunch of kids from the fifties!'

'Well, in a sense, yes,' said Jasper. 'We find mysteries and we solve them, bringing the criminals to their knees if necessary.'

I looked to Charlie.

'I just like puzzles.' He shrugged again.

'And you want me to join you?' I said.

'You've already bested my second-in-command in a battle of knowledge and deciphered the invitation in one night. I'd say you are a prime candidate.'

I looked around at them all. They weren't exactly the cool kids that I wanted to hang out with, but maybe I had to face the fact that I wasn't cool-kid material.

'What mysteries have you solved, then?' I asked. Michelle went red and looked at the floor, Charlie let out a huge laugh again, while Jasper straightened his glasses and smiled proudly.

'Our combined skills have been used to find a missing person and solve a mathematical conundrum.'

'He means,' said Michelle, 'that we found his sister's hamster when it escaped from its cage and we worked out how to get as many right-angled-triangle sandwiches as possible out of one sliced loaf.'

I stopped myself from laughing.

'Wow. MI5 must be quaking in their boots.'

'The point is, the group is still developing, still hungry for its first big case and your skills would complete it,' said Jasper, getting tetchy. 'I've taken a great risk by revealing ourselves to you. I don't

35

know much about you. You could be working for the enemy for all I know.'

'You have an enemy?'

'No,' said Charlie. 'But we plan to get one. Come on, mate, it'll be a laugh.'

I looked to Michelle, who was suspiciously quiet.

'Don't look at me, I'm not begging,' she said, her arms folded.

'Are you still sore that I beat you at that prime number thing?'

Michelle's face darkened.

'Absolutely not. I slipped up on one number, that's all. I hardly think that makes you Codebuster material,' she spat. 'However, we could use a good cryptographer, so that's why I slipped you the card.' Charlie looked confused. Michelle sighed. 'It means "code-breaker", Charlie, we've been over this.'

I turned away from them while I thought about it. It was nice to be asked to be a part of a group. Charlie seemed cool, Michelle was a little frosty perhaps and Jasper was downright bonkers, but they were the only friends I was likely to get at the moment. Old geeky Jackson would have jumped at the chance, but I was trying to leave him behind. I was cool Jax now – what would *he* do?

'Sorry,' I said. 'I'm going to pass.'

Jasper's smile faded, but he quickly regained his cool. He stood up straight and gave me a short, sharp nod.

'Very well. I'm sorry to have wasted your time. I trust you will keep our organisation top secret?'

I stepped forward and shook his hand.

'You can trust me. I won't be telling *anyone* about this.'

I turned to leave, but my bag spilled open, the contents falling on the floor. Typical. I can't even make a cool exit. Charlie dashed forward and helped me pick up my things.

'Nice gloves. You play in goal?' he said.

'Yeah. Playing tonight actually, in the park next to the school. You can come if you want?'

Charlie's face dropped.

'You're playing with the Bragg brothers?' he said. I nodded. He put my stuff back in my bag and laid his hand on my shoulder. 'It was nice knowing you, mate.'

I left the chemistry lab feeling very confused and a little scared. As I went, I heard Jasper whisper to the others:

'Don't worry, he'll be back.'

Chapter Four

I went through the day with a sense of unease and slight dread. When school was over, I seriously thought about going straight home, but I told myself it wouldn't be that bad. After all, why would the Bragg brothers invite me to play with them if they were going to beat me up? A little voice inside my head said they'd invited me to play *because* they wanted to beat me up. I was the only one stupid enough to go to their park, so I would be the one they'd pick on. I told the little voice to shut up and forced myself into the park, where I walked slowly down the path.

Dan (or Dave) welcomed me by giving me a friendly punch on the arm, then Dom (or possibly Dan) jokingly kicked me in the back of the knees so I fell to the ground. We all laughed about it, but thinking back I can't quite remember what was so funny. We started to play, me in a goal made of coats and school bags (my school bag anyway, it turns out that the Braggs were excluded from Bletchley Grange after giving a teacher a nervous breakdown). It was a good kickabout, but the brothers didn't seem bothered about passing the ball or playing against each other. They just liked belting the ball as hard as they could at me and then making me go and get it from the trees behind me.

I was soon caked in mud, my T-shirt sticking to my body and my feet weighing a tonne from all the mud that my shoes had collected. The ball came sailing past me and I hardly had time to scream before all three brothers came running at me, knocking me down.

'Bundle!'

I winced as Dan, Dom and Dave hurled themselves on top of me, crushing me into the soft, muddy ground. They lay there for a bit, laughing like goons as they knocked the wind out of me.

'Break! Time for chips!' one shouted. I couldn't tell which one, as I could only see mud at this point. They climbed off me and grabbed their coats. I was glad of the call for chips – I was starving.

'Good game, Jax. Nice keeping,' said... oh, I don't know, one of them. They all looked the same.

'Thanks,' I said, still lying flat on the ground, winded and unable to move. 'So... same time tomorrow?' This was great. Only my second day at school and I was already forging firm friendships with some, well, *interesting* characters. They were a bit rough, and occasionally violent, but they'd be great to have as mates.

They all laughed.

'Don't take this the wrong way, Jax, but if you ever come to our park again, we might have to beat you up a bit.'

I was confused.

'Yeah, you're all right, but we've got a reputation to keep. If word gets out we've let anyone come in here, everyone'll think we've gone soft.'

'So... you just wanted someone you could stick in goal and bundle on?' I said, slightly dazed.

'Yep. Now remember – not a word to anyone. But if you ever need a favour, you know where to find us. See ya!'

They all cheerily waved goodbye while I lay in the mud, thinking over what they had said. I had spent the last few hours running about, getting balls kicked at my head and taking a light thumping, for nothing. I wasn't allowed to come to the park again, or tell anyone I'd played football with the Braggs. I didn't even get any chips! I was beginning to realise what a fool I'd been.

'Are you all right?'

The voice came from the path next to me. I managed to lift my head to see an old man with a walking stick looking at me. I propped myself up on my elbows.

'Fine, thank you.' I got to my feet and walked over to the path, looking like a mud monster from the swamp. 'Just having a bit of a kickabout.'

The old man smiled. He was probably around eighty years old and wore a trench coat with a trilby hat. He let me walk alongside him, but I was careful not to brush into him and get him muddy too. He walked with a limp and I was only able to go slowly due to my aching muscles and heavy muddy boots, so our pace matched perfectly.

'If I may say, you didn't seem to be having much fun,' he said.

'I'm not supposed to be having fun, I'm supposed to be making friends,' I said. I realised how absurd that sounded and began to laugh. The man joined me, his laugh a polite one.

'You must be new in town,' said the man.

'Does it show?' He smiled again.

'Eager to impress new friends. A new school bag and goalkeeping gloves. And everyone knows this park belongs to the Bragg brothers. A rookie mistake coming in here if ever I saw one.'

I could have felt insulted by that I suppose, but he was right.

'Are you a detective or something?'

'Goodness me, no.' He smiled. 'I just notice things.' He seemed to drift off for a moment, gazing at the trees around him and the changing leaves of autumn. 'It always seemed to me that real friends were those who have fun *with* you, not make fun *of* you. I remember a time when I was on a mission with a group of men who I assumed were my friends.'

'You were in the army?' I asked. He stopped, stood to attention and gave a serious salute, which he followed with a smile.

'A captain, no less. After the war we had national service and we all had to serve for two years. I stayed on for a while longer, always a glutton for punishment.

'These two men – boys, really – started to mess around. We were walking along a path through the jungle and we were meant to keep to it, but they got a bit rough, pushing and shoving, larking about. They elbowed me off the path, into the undergrowth.

'There's no way to describe the sound of stepping on a land mine. It makes a simple *click* of course, but in that tiny sound you know you have just seconds to act.'

I stared at him, my mouth wide open in amazement.

'You stepped on a land mine? What happened?'

The old man raised his walking stick and gave his right leg a great big whack with the tip. It clanged like an old bell, a gritty, metallic sound.

'I got sent home and recovered well, thankfully just losing the one leg. But it goes to show how picking the wrong friends can go badly wrong, eh?'

My mind raced. Okay, the Braggs weren't about to blow my leg off (I hope), but I could see they didn't have my best interests at heart.

'What happened to the other soldiers?'

'Court-martialled, then discharged. One became a vacuum-cleaner salesman, the other a very wealthy banker in London,' he said. 'I never even received an apology.'

'Wow. Are you still angry?'

He shrugged. 'It was over fifty years ago. There's only so long you can hold a grudge. I learnt my lesson though. I only ever did the things that I enjoyed from then on, never pretending for someone else, or when trying to make a friend.'

We came to the park gates, and stopped.

'My grandad would have liked you. He loved army stories, anything about the war.' I started to go, but turned back quickly and gave a salute.

'At ease, soldier,' the old man said with a twinkle in his eye. I knew I couldn't go straight back home covered in mud – Mum would kill me if I got it on our new carpet – so I popped back to school where I had seen an outside tap next to the PE changing rooms. I got most of the mud off my shoes, then noticed the cleaners were still at work in the school hall so I nipped inside to get a can of lemonade from the vending machine.

As the can dropped to the floor of the machine, I heard raised voices coming from outside the hall.

'We are not getting the police involved. The embarrassment would be too much to bear.'

I inched forward to the door and peered out of the tall thin pane of glass set into it. Mr Kirrin, the head, was out there with Miss Almond, our maths teacher.

'But the kids worked hard for that trophy. Jasper especially. If we don't recover it, they'll be crushed,' said Miss Almond.

My ears pricked up at the mention of Jasper's name. I moved my head to see what they were looking at. In front of them was the school trophy cabinet, laden with sports medals and awards. The teachers were looking directly ahead at a space in the cabinet.

'I still can't work out how they stole it,' said Mr Kirrin. 'This is always kept locked with a combination padlock. Three numbers, known only to myself.'

'That's one thousand possible combinations. They must have known what they were doing.'

The teachers walked off towards the head's office. I carefully opened the door and walked over to the trophy cabinet. I had no idea if I was meant to be there or not, but as the teachers seemed to be searching for a thief I thought I probably shouldn't make myself appear too suspicious. Like, say, hanging around school after hours, looking like I'd just dug a grave.

The trophy cabinet was locked with a padlock, just as Mr Kirrin had said, and no glass had been smashed. No other trophies had been taken either, just the maths one. I looked through the glass at the empty space. At the front stood a small card:

Regional Mathematics Trophy
won by Jasper Newton and Michelle Chang

I remembered the head's announcement from yesterday – it was Jasper and Michelle's trophy that had gone missing! There wasn't much I could do about it, so I turned to leave, walking past reception, where a giant plasma screen hung on the wall. This normally played a slideshow of school notices and displayed Mr Kirrin's morning announcements. As I passed, it flickered into life. I stopped as I saw what it was showing:

AMBCZSQRCPQ AMKC MSR RM NJYW!

Another code. The letters scrolled slowly across the screen and I quickly reached for a pad of paper from my bag to note it down. I stared at the screen for a few more moments, checking that I had got each letter exactly right. Someone was playing a game. They'd stolen a trophy and left a code in its place.

I couldn't resist the challenge. I just *had* to crack the code.

Chapter Five

I got up early again and raced past Mum to get to school. As I went out of the door, she shouted after me, telling me not to get caked in mud again. There was no chance of that. I knew who I was going to meet today and I doubted we'd be playing football.

I made my way to the old chemistry lab and burst through the doors. Jasper and Michelle were sitting opposite each other on a desk, doing Sudoku puzzles. They were each deep in concentration, their pens whipping over the squares faster than a greyhound that badly needed the toilet. Charlie stood between them with a stopwatch. As I approached, he smiled, but made a sign for me to keep quiet. I only had to wait another few seconds before Jasper smacked his hand down on the table.

'Done!' he said with a grin. Michelle threw down her pen in frustration.

'New record for you,' said Charlie, showing Jasper the stopwatch. 'Four minutes and twenty seconds. That's crazy.'

'Just takes practice,' said Jasper. He saw me standing there, seemingly for the first time. 'Mr Hilbert! To what do we owe this pleasure? I thought you wanted nothing to do with our organisation?'

I grabbed the pad from my bag.

'I'm bringing you your first real mystery.' I explained about my eavesdropping on the teachers and the missing trophy. I showed them the code I had noted down.

'I saw Miss Almond as I came in this morning,' said Jasper. 'She said the trophy had been sent away to be engraved.'

'And the plasma screen has a big "out of order" sign taped to it,' said Michelle.

'I guess they can't get it to stop displaying the code.' I shrugged. 'Or they don't even recognise it *is* a code. They probably think the computer's crashed so they've unplugged it.'

Charlie took the pad from me.

'So what does it say?'

'It's –' Jasper and I both spoke at the same time.

'Please, go ahead,' he said. I could see he wanted to show off by deciphering the code himself, but I think I was being tested again.

'The code is called a Caesar Shift. It's fairly simple and has been used since Roman times. You take each letter and replace it with the letter a number of places before or after it in the alphabet. In this case, two places after.'

'So all I have to do is take the letter on the code, count two letters ahead of it in the alphabet, and that's the real letter?' said Charlie. I nodded 'So... A becomes C? And B becomes D?'

'Yep,' I said. 'See if you can solve it.'

Charlie grabbed a pen and soon had the message deciphered.

'Well, I can safely say that someone knows the identity of our "secret" group,' he said finally. He threw the pad on the desk, showing the code, followed by the decoded message:

AMBCZSQRCPQ AMKC MSR RM NJYW!
CODEBUSTERS COME OUT TO PLAY!

'Who would do this?' said Michelle. I shrugged.

51

'Someone with time on their hands and an axe to grind,' I said. 'Maybe you've upset someone?'

'Well, that could be anyone,' said Michelle. Jasper shot her a look. 'Oh, come on, Jasper! You're a borderline genius, but when it comes to tact and friendship, you do tend to make people a bit angry.'

Jasper raised an eyebrow.

'What do you mean "borderline"? I *am* a genius.'

'And so modest...' laughed Charlie.

I sat down next to Michelle and we all racked our brains for who the culprit could be. Of course, I'd only been at the school for a couple of days, so I wasn't much help.

'It's useless. No one fits the profile,' said Michelle after a few minutes.

'We have a profile?' I said.

'What, like on Facebook?' offered Charlie. Michelle sighed.

'*Criminal* profile. You work out what type of person could have committed the crime and then narrow down your suspects from there. We're looking for someone with a grudge, maybe someone who doesn't like us. Someone with the cheek to steal the trophy and leave a note to taunt us.'

We all looked at each other suspiciously.

'Wow, Michelle. Someone's been reading a lot of detective novels,' I said, breaking the tension.

'Actually, my mum's a criminologist.'

Charlie let out a gasp. 'Has she been in prison and stuff?'

'*Criminologist*, Charlie. She *studies* criminals, she's not a criminal herself.'

All this time, Jasper had been pacing up and down the lab, his eyes closed and his fingers massaging his temples. All of a sudden he let out a blood-curdling shriek, like he had trapped his thumb in a drawer. We all nearly jumped out of our skins.

'Aha! I've been such an idiot!' he said, a smile forming on his face. The smile was replaced quickly by a crazy giggle. It was the kind of laugh you'd hear in a film, when the baddie was explaining their fiendish plan. The rest of us exchanged worried glances.

'So you know who did it?' asked Charlie.

'No! No, of course not! But don't you see? That's the point!' He giggled. We stared at him blankly. 'Never mind. Of course you don't get it, you poor idiotic fools! But you will, you all will! Meet me here after school. We're going on a field trip!'

He grabbed his school bag (actually, it was a briefcase) and walked out of the lab. A few moments later he popped his head around the door.

'Can I assume, Mr Hilbert, that you will be joining the Codebusters after all?'

I looked at Charlie and Michelle, who smiled at me with expectant faces.

'Well, just for now,' I said. 'You're lucky I'm rubbish in goal.'

'Excellent! Welcome aboard! Sport's loss is our gain,' he said and darted off again. Michelle, Charlie and I sat quietly for a moment in confusion.

'Is he always like that?' I asked. They nodded slowly.

I sighed. What on earth had I let myself in for?

Chapter Six

I got through the day without any major embarrassments, largely due to the fact that I wasn't trying (and failing) to be cool. Charlie met up with me at lunch (with a lunch box that looked like he had ram-raided a sweet shop) and we chatted about normal things: films, telly, football and stuff. He was a cool guy and we had loads in common. We both liked superhero movies, car chases and things that blow up. He had a particular love of old kung-fu movies and quiz shows where he could show off his brain. I got the impression that he felt he was the least intelligent of the group, just because Michelle and Jasper liked to show off a bit, but it soon became clear that he had a photographic memory and an amazing ability to navigate spaces and mazes.

When I tried to talk about the Codebusters, he just shook his head and tapped the side of his nose. When we met after lessons in the old chemistry lab, I asked him about it.

'Jasper might seem a bit weird for keeping the Codebusters top secret, but he has his reasons. And now we seem to have our first real enemy, it's probably best to keep quiet about it all in public,' said Charlie. I nodded.

'So we only talk about codes and stuff inside this lab?'

'Yep. Oh, and we call it HQ,' he said. 'Jasper insists.'

As if summoned by the mention of his name, Jasper poked his head round the door.

'Come on, chaps! No time to waste!'

We followed him, Michelle joining us, as he walked out of the school and across the sports field to a small clump of trees on the school grounds.

'Is he going to kill us and bury us out here?' I joked. Charlie laughed.

'That's the problem with Jasper,' said Michelle, her face deadly serious. 'You can never tell.' We stopped laughing.

We came to a fence that marked the boundary of the school's land, and Jasper turned to face us.

'Is this where the secret entrance to your bat cave is?' I asked.

Jasper ignored me and approached the fence. With a light thump, he loosened a board, which slid out of the way to make a hole big enough to slip through.

'Ladies first,' said Jasper, holding back the board. Michelle went through, followed by Charlie. I hesitated.

'What's the matter, Mr Hilbert? Don't you trust me?'

I eyed him carefully as I slid through the fence.

I found myself in a beautiful garden with rose bushes, apple trees and a vegetable patch outside a pretty thatched cottage. Standing at the back of the garden, picking blackberries from a bush, was a familiar face.

'Well, well, well! The troops have arrived with a new recruit,' said an old man. It was the same man I had seen at the park the previous day. He laughed, and I saluted again.

'You know the Professor?' said Michelle.

'We met yesterday,' I said. 'Although I thought you said you were a captain.'

The man limped over to join us, offering the fresh berries.

'I have been many things in my life. My full name would be Captain Sir Alastair Horatio Turing PhD, but I've only ever been known as "Sparky", or "Hopalong" –' he tapped his tin leg – 'and now "the Professor".'

I tasted the sweet blackberries as he led us through to his house. While he prepared some tea and cake, Jasper explained what we were doing there.

'The Professor is a founder member of the Codebusters. He used to be a professor of mathematics and when he retired he became a governor of the school. When I first arrived at Bletchley Grange he noticed my considerable talent for codebreaking and detection and encouraged me to form the group. During my first year, it was only made up of him and myself. And now Miss Chang and Mr Babbage have joined us he has become a sort of "advisor". He has the most sparkling intellect and a very active mind.'

'Yeah, and he serves wicked cakes,' said Charlie.

The Professor arrived with a tray of tea, fondant fancies and Battenberg cake.

'So young Jasper here has managed to charm you into the gang. How're they treating you?' he asked.

'Very well, sir,' I said. 'I'm eight hours in and have no complaints so far.'

'We have a thief at school, Professor,' said Jasper, getting straight to the point.

'Good gracious, how terrible!' said the Professor. 'And yet, how exciting! Do tell all!'

We told him about the stolen trophy, the cover-up by the teachers and the code left to taunt us. When we had finished, the Professor looked amazed. He took the pad of paper with the code on it from Charlie and stared at it for a few moments.

'Goodness. Do you think it could be –?'

'That's what I wanted you to confirm, sir,' said Jasper.

'I can see no other way. It must be –'

'That's what I was afraid of.'

Charlie, Michelle and I looked back and forth between the two boffins like we were watching a game of table tennis.

'Will someone talk in complete sentences please? Some of us can't read minds,' said Charlie.

'Hmm? Oh yes, of course,' said the Professor. He rose from his chair and stood at the fireplace, staring at a photo of what looked like a younger version of himself dressed in a captain's uniform. 'I'm afraid I haven't told you my complete story. After I was invalided out of the army, I used my war pension to put myself through university, studying maths and codes. I was later invited back by the military to join MI6.'

'The Secret Service?' said Charlie, his mouth full of cake.

'Exactly. I worked abroad for years, helping with the Cold War, and when I came back I was retained as an advisor.'

'What's this got to do with a missing trophy?' said Michelle.

'Throughout my time at MI6, we were dogged with messages from an unknown person, who we named Elgar.'

'Like the composer?' I asked. 'The one who wrote "Land of Hope and Glory"?'

'Yes. The real Elgar left a message after his death written in a code that has never been broken. *Our* Elgar left notes similar to this –' he waved the sheet of paper – 'taunting us, playing games, stealing things. We never found out who it was, although we were able to crack most of the problems he left. And now it seems that you have an Elgar of your own to deal with.'

We all paused for thought and helped ourselves to more cake.

'So you managed to solve the clues he left? And recover the things he stole? Back then, I mean,' I said, trying to get my head round the situation.

'Yes, mostly.'

'So what sort of clues or messages can we expect?' I asked.

'More codes, certainly,' said the Professor. 'Puzzles, riddles, that sort of thing. Some could be deliciously hard, some devilishly dangerous. Some will seem easy, but will have a sting in the tail. Each clue will lead on to the next, like a treasure trail, and the stakes will get higher every step of the way. I remember a time we saved the *Mona Lisa*. It was left dangling over a vat of chicken soup, and had we not solved the clue –'

'Elgar stole the *Mona Lisa*?' interrupted Michelle. 'Why?'

The Professor smiled.

'We never knew! Not to sell it, certainly. He seemed to like the thrill of the chase, that's all.'

We sat in silence (except for the sound of Charlie munching his way through the cakes). So this is what we were up against. A mischievous prankster intent on playing with us like a cat plays with a mouse. Michelle looked scared. Jasper looked thrilled.

'So how do we beat him? What do we do next?'

'You wait,' said the Professor. 'You wait and you play the game.'

Jasper stood and grinned.

'The Codebusters are ready, sir! Bring it on!'

We all burst out laughing, Charlie spraying cake across the room. It was a very un-Jasperish thing to say.

'Very good, Jasper, but let me say this: while it may seem like a good challenge, *fun* even, never underestimate Elgar. The moment you think it's a fun little jape, he'll turn the tables and you may find yourselves in serious danger.'

Jasper grabbed his briefcase and shook the Professor's hand.

'Do not fear, sir, we're made of strong stuff! Codebusters, we have work to do. Mr Hilbert, we still need to train you up. Come on, chop-chop!'

He started to leave and we got up to join him. Somehow he had a way of speaking to us that made us feel like he was our head teacher and we had been summoned to detention.

'Thank you for your hospitality,' said Michelle to the Professor as we passed.

'Cheers for the cake, Prof!' said Charlie.

As I left, the Professor put a hand on my shoulder and spoke to me quietly.

'Jax, you've made a good decision. I think you'll find this group a better choice of friends than the Bragg brothers,' he said with a kind smile. 'Can you do one thing for me? Keep an eye on Jasper, will you? He's a little too hungry for glory. I've seen men in similar conditions get into one or two spots of bother, and while he may think he's a sergeant major, he may need reminding once in a while that he's actually an eleven-year-old boy.'

He smiled. It was quite touching that he was so concerned for Jasper.

'Of course, Captain,' I said. I saluted him once more, and followed the rest of the Codebusters down the garden path.

Chapter Seven

I stayed late after school the next day and went to the old chemistry lab (sorry, HQ). Mum was getting suspicious about why I was spending so much time at school, as I'd never been keen to go before, but I told her I was meeting up with friends, which I was, I suppose. When I arrived Jasper was already there. I was beginning to think that he never went home.

'Ah, Mr Hilbert!'

'You know, Jasper, you *can* call me Jax.'

Jasper thought about it. 'No. No, I don't think I can,' he said, shaking his head. I was suddenly aware that this was the first time Jasper and I had been alone together and I had no idea what to talk to him about. Luckily, Jasper was blind to this sort of social awkwardness and he launched into his sergeant major persona. 'I've taken the liberty of preparing a test.'

He laid out two sheets of paper on a workbench, with a pen beside each. Charlie and Michelle entered together.

'Wassup, busters?' said Charlie, giving me a high five like the nerdiest rapper ever. He may be a pale chubby maths geek, but I thought he was a great guy. He didn't seem to care what people thought of him, and that's pretty cool in my book.

'Mr Babbage, take a seat,' said Jasper.

'Ooh, a test?'

'A *timed* test, no less. Mr Hilbert, you've beaten my second in command with your knowledge, cracked codes, and now you must face our physical puzzle expert.'

'That's me,' said Charlie, grinning.

'How come you're so good at mazes and things?' I asked. Charlie shrugged.

'Just am. My dad's a taxi driver. Did you know that all London cabbies have to do The Knowledge? They have to learn all the streets in London and the shortest route between them.' I nodded. 'I could do that by the time I was five.'

I whistled, impressed. Charlie was obviously very proud of his skill.

'Gentlemen – one maze, one opponent. The fastest to get from the entrance to the exit wins.'

'Good luck,' said Michelle.

'Thanks,' said Charlie and I together.

'On your marks.'

I picked up my pencil and took a deep breath.

'Get set.'

I looked at Charlie, who was enjoying the tension. He winked at me.

'GO!'

We flipped our pages over at the same time, and started to trace our way through the maze. I could see Charlie whizzing along, but I told myself to concentrate. I imagined myself into the maze on the page and suddenly I was speeding through it too! Eventually I hit the exit and I banged my fist on the table.

'Finished!'

They all looked at me, amazed.

'Impossible!' said Charlie. Michelle picked up my piece of paper and checked it.

'It's right. We have a winner!' She held my arm aloft and Jasper applauded.

'I don't believe it,' said Charlie. I glanced down at his maze. He was only about halfway through.

'No hard feelings, eh, Charlie?' Charlie just shrugged. He got up and grabbed his bag, leaving without saying a word.

'Hmm, meeting adjourned, then,' said Jasper. 'I thought that would take longer.'

I felt bad about Charlie going off like that. He had looked crushed. I looked at the empty doorway and Michelle appeared by my side.

'Do you think he'll be okay?' I asked.

'Charlie? Of course,' said Michelle. 'He's just never been beaten before, that's all. He'll bounce back. Come on, let's walk home.'

I did a double take.

'What, together?' I said. Michelle nodded slowly, like I was being an idiot. It was the first time she had spoken to me without an undertone of sarcasm in her voice.

'What about you, Jasper?' she said. 'Coming with us?'

Jasper was clearing away his pens and paper. He looked flustered and pushed his glasses back up his nose.

'Hmm? No thank you. I've got a few things to do here first.'

'No worries. See ya tomorrow.'

We walked out of school and along the path past the park. I did my best to make polite conversation, but what do you talk about with an ice-cool maths queen? I decided to stick with a reliable subject.

'So what's the story with Jasper? He's kind of... I don't know... serious?'

'That's just him. I don't know much about him really. He's our age, but he's in the year above. He *is* very serious, and a genius as well. He was put forward a year because he was so smart and I don't think he made friends very well at first, so he created the Codebusters with the Professor. Sergeant major suits him, don't you think?'

I laughed. 'I can't imagine him *taking* orders, if that's what you mean. What about you?'

'No, I can't either.'

'Actually, I meant, what's your story?' Michelle gave me a sideways smile.

'I'm not sure I've got one. I –'

'BUNDLE!'

Just then I was jumped on and forced to the ground, where two boys sat on me and bounced up and down.

'GEEK ATTACK!'

They were large boys and I recognised them as the numbskulls that had taken the mickey out of me on the first day after maths.

'ZE-RO! ZE-RO! ZE-RO!' they chanted like robots.

'Neil, get off him! Pack it in, Jimmy!' screamed Michelle.

'Shut it, Nerd Girl! You're just lucky you're not at the bottom,' said Neil, the larger of the two. After a few scuffles and light punches to the ribs, they got off me and legged it down the road, laughing.

'Idiots!' shouted Michelle after them.

I lay there for a few moments, slightly winded and deeply embarrassed about being beaten up in front of Michelle.

'Are you hurt?' said Michelle, crouching down beside me.

'Just my pride,' I laughed, struggling to my feet.

'Your phone –' said Michelle, picking up my new smart phone from the pavement. 'Do you think they were trying to steal it?' I shook my head.

'Nah. That was a standard Geek Attack. A light beating to enforce who's in charge.'

'All because you're better than them at maths? Do you get that often? It's never happened to me.'

'More than I'd like,' I smiled. 'Now, where were we?'

'I believe you were trying to get me to tell you something about myself?'

'Of course. Now make it good. I just took a few punches for you.'

'Ooh, my hero,' she said. It was thick with sarcasm, but the good, friendly kind. It seemed that all I had to do to break the ice with Michelle was get jumped on by a couple of goons. I made a mental note to remember that for next time...

She chatted easily about herself. Her parents had moved here from China when she was three. Her mum and dad both worked at the university in the neighbouring town. Her mum taught criminology and her dad taught maths.

'No wonder you're a Codebuster, with that background.'

'I suppose. They didn't force me to learn or anything, I just picked it up. They keep threatening to send me to a better school, but it would mean boarding and I want to stay here with my family.'

We came to Michelle's gate.

'Thanks for walking me back. Those idiots shook me up a bit,' she said.

'No probs. It's nice to have a friend in town. I don't really know anyone –'

My phone started to ring and vibrate in my pocket.

'Who's that?'

'Beats me,' I said. 'Like I said, I don't know anyone here. And it's a new phone; no one even has my number.'

I fished the phone out of my pocket, tapped the 'answer' button and set it to speakerphone. Michelle and I leaned in to hear more clearly over the sound of cars and the autumn wind.

'WELCOME,' said a tinny, electronic voice. 'DO YOU WANT TO PLAY A GAME?'

'He's disguising his voice, using a computer,' said Michelle.

'PAY ATTENTION:

TWO LEFTS AND A RIGHT WON'T MAKE A WRONG,

BUT TWO MORE LEFTS WILL MAKE A SONG.

MARCH TO THE LEFT, THEN STRAIGHT AHEAD,

FIND A CLUE ABOVE YOUR HEAD.'

Click. He had hung up, very briskly.

'Directions. Did you get them all?' I said.

'Left, left, right. Left, left, left, straight ahead and up.'

'You can do that from memory?' I said, amazed.

'Of course. Can't you?' Michelle smiled. 'Not really. I wrote it on my hand.' She showed me an ink-stained palm.

'It's hardly a fair test, is it? We don't know where to start. Any ideas?'

'Don't look at me. You're the new "spatial and physical" expert.'

Maybe I was, but the directions meant nothing to me, especially as I didn't know the neighbourhood. I stared at the directions on Michelle's hand, but I couldn't begin to find the starting point. We tried walking from where we were, but ended up in someone's garden, in the middle of the flowerbed.

After we'd run away from an angry gardener with a sharp trowel, we stopped outside some shops. We sat on the kerb, breathless.

'This is hopeless,' I said. 'I don't know who I was trying to fool. I just got lucky with that maze before.'

'We need help,' said Michelle. I nodded.

'We need Charlie.'

Chapter Eight

Charlie lived in a small terraced house a few streets away. Michelle led us there, and I hoped that turning up out of the blue wouldn't make him more upset. Clearly I wasn't his favourite person at that moment, but we needed him to help solve the clue. I was enjoying being part of a gang. I had forgotten about trying to be the cool kid in school and it was fun hanging out with the Codebusters. I hoped Charlie would be okay with me so we could start cracking the new clue.

We knocked on the door and Charlie's mum answered. She seemed genuinely pleased to see us and ushered us up to his room. We passed picture after picture of Charlie on the stairs, from baby photos to school portraits, each one with his trademark floppy blond hair. It appeared he was an only child and it was obvious that his mum doted on him.

'You want any cake, or crisps?' she offered. 'Squash? Tea? Coffee? Sandwiches? It's no trouble!'

We politely refused all offers of refreshment and Michelle called out to let Charlie know we were there. He looked confused to see us.

'Hi, Charlie,' I said, hoping he wouldn't tell us to go away. 'I know you don't like me much at the moment, but we need your help –'

'There's no one else who can do it,' added Michelle.

'I just got lucky before, but now we need your skills, and quickly.'

Charlie looked at us blankly for a few seconds, then burst into a smile, followed by his usual hearty laugh.

'Blimey, I've only been gone an hour and a half! What sort of trouble have you got yourself into now?'

I breathed easy. I should have known he wouldn't be cross for long. He was just too nice a guy. He invited us into his room, a messy place with football posters and hand-drawn mazes tacked to the walls, which had been decorated in old Disney wallpaper. He must have lived in that room since he was a baby, but they had never got round to redecorating. He kicked a few pairs of pants off the bed and we sat down, Michelle pulling a disgusted face.

'It's nice to have a fan club. Sorry about earlier, at HQ. Just came as a bit of a shock that's all. I didn't mean to get childish about it, but... well, puzzles are kind of *my thing*, you know?'

He looked a bit sad, so I tried to cheer him up.

'And have we got a puzzle for you! I had a call just now from our favourite prankster.'

I explained the clue and Michelle showed him the rapidly scrawled directions on her hand.

'Sorry, means nothing to me.' Charlie shrugged. 'Like you said, without a starting point, or even a general location, it's meaningless.'

'We must be able to think of *something*,' said Michelle. 'We can't be at a dead end already.'

'What *exactly* did Elgar say?' Charlie asked. Between us, we managed to note down the rhyming riddle from memory. Mrs Babbage arrived with some drinks and biscuits ('I know you said you didn't want nothing, but I decided you were just being polite.') and Charlie sat trying to decipher the clue.

'That's more like it,' he said, with half a custard cream in his mouth. 'There's a clue in the riddle, see? *Another two lefts will make a song*. It's strange sayings like that which scream "clue" at you.' It was funny watching Charlie trying to puzzle it out. He went from a jokey clown to an ultra-serious cryptology expert in a matter of seconds. 'I think it's time I showed you something Jasper and I have been working on.'

He went to the corner of his room, where his laptop lay on a desk. He sat down and tapped on the keyboard while Michelle and I crowded round. The screen flashed and a program appeared on the screen. It looked sophisticated, a blur of code running in the background, with a few icons in front.

'Meet OSCAR, the other member of the Codebusters.'

'Who?'

'OSCAR. It stands for Online System for Cipher Analysis and Research. It's where we can put our combined knowledge of codes and puzzles and let the computer work out the clues.'

I looked blankly at him.

'It's like Jasper's brain, but in a computer,' he said. I nodded, understanding finally.

'How come I didn't know about this?' said Michelle.

'Jasper wanted to wait until it was ready and do a grand dramatic unveiling. You know what he's like.'

Charlie explained how OSCAR worked, most of which went over my head. He demonstrated by feeding in all the information we knew about Elgar and the clues so far. He typed in the riddle, and we watched the program beep and buzz while it worked out what it meant.

'It's matching up the directions in the riddle to all of the map data it can find on the Internet,' explained Charlie. 'It knows that Elgar has access to many of the same places that we do, so it's concentrating on the school. That's probably how Elgar was able to steal the trophy without being noticed and hack into the plasma screen to make it display the code.'

'You think Elgar is a student?' I said. Up until then I had imagined Elgar as some kind of creepy mad scientist in a white coat, laughing manically at our attempts to solve his riddles. The idea that it could be a student like us was frightening. I could have passed him in the corridor loads of times and not even known.

'That's our best guess. Anyway, if I'm right –'

The laptop let out a shrill *bing!* and the screen flashed with the words: 'Match found'. Charlie clicked a button and a map spun on to the screen. I recognised it as the school, the same map I had been given, but with a red line where the computer had traced the directions.

'Yes!' said Charlie, helping himself to a bourbon biscuit. 'It's the school. The bit about a song in the riddle is talking about the music room, making the starting place the trophy cabinet.'

I looked at the screen, and was amazed with the system Charlie and Jasper had rigged up.

'Wow. I want one!' I laughed. Just then, my phone beeped in my pocket.

'You've got one,' said Charlie. 'I just sent you an app that allows you to use OSCAR any time of the day or night.'

I checked my phone and sure enough there was a little blue icon on the home screen. I tapped it and the same snazzy blue screen popped up.

'Cool!'

'You can even talk with the other members of the group using the communications button. It scrambles the signal so Elgar shouldn't be able to listen in.'

Michelle pouted. 'Don't I get one?' Charlie grinned and tapped a button. Michelle's phone beeped seconds later. 'Thank you!' she smiled.

We got distracted for a few minutes playing with OSCAR on our phones, messing about like kids with a new toy, which is, I suppose, what we were. It was great to let loose with Charlie and Michelle. None of my other friends would talk about computers or maths stuff with me. Then I remembered I didn't have any other friends...

'Er, guys,' called Michelle eventually, staring at the map on the screen. 'You know we said Elgar has access to the same places we do?'

'Yeah,' said Charlie and I together.

'Well, I think he might have a bit more access than we first thought.' She traced her finger over the map to the end of the red line.

'That's...' said Charlie.

'What?' I said.

'Yep,' said Michelle.

'But how?'

I looked between the two of them and sighed. 'Somebody? Anybody? What are you talking about?'

Charlie put his finger on the flashing dot on the map, the place that Elgar's clue had led us to.

'That,' he said, 'is the head teacher's office.'

I looked as the map became clearer.

'And that's where the next clue is?' They nodded. 'How are we meant to get in there?'

Charlie sat down, looking defeated already.

'I have no idea.'

Chapter Nine

The dinner hall reeked of chips and sweat, as it doubled as the school gym in lesson time. Outside it was tipping it down, forcing all the students to hang around inside, taking as long as possible over their food. I had a packed lunch and managed to find the rest of the Codebusters to sit with in the crowded hall. It was cold, the first really chilly day of autumn, and I had somehow forgotten to wear a hoodie. Michelle had sensibly worn a cardigan, Charlie wore a sweater with a superhero across the front, and even Jasper wore an argyle jumper underneath his blazer.

'All right, guys? Nippy isn't it?' I said.

'I'd get used to it if I were you,' said Charlie. 'Mr Kirrin never turns the heating on until late in the year and he's got this new eco-boiler thing now that's going to burn up all the school's rubbish, so he's going to be a mega-scrooge when it comes to energy.'

'We're a "green" school now, apparently,' said Michelle. She ducked as a chip flew past her head. 'I wish they'd get rid of *that* rubbish.' She signalled to the table opposite, where the chip had come from. It was Neil and Jimmy, the same two goons who had jumped me in the street. They were throwing chips at Michelle, then when she turned round, acting all innocent like it wasn't them. When she turned back, they'd laugh their heads off. Michelle looked really annoyed.

'Do you want me to have a word?' I said.

'No! Don't rise to them, just ignore it.' I did what she asked, but wasn't sure that was the best way to get rid of them.

'Hello? Am I the only sane one here? We're in the middle of a major mission and we're chatting about the weather and projectile potatoes,' said Jasper. 'Can we deal with the matter in hand?' He picked a chip out of his mass of curly hair, trying to look dignified.

'What "matter"? It's over, we've hit a dead end,' said Charlie. 'There's no way we can get into the head's office. And even if we did, it says, "look up". What are we meant to do, read the clue off the ceiling?'

Jasper threw down the rogue chip in disgust.

'Is that the Codebuster spirit? Giving up at the first hurdle? Come on, team! We're the most intelligent crew in this school! We can work out a way of defeating this monster!'

We all grunted unenthusiastically. A chip sailed past Michelle's head again and landed in her yogurt. I half stood to go and deal with Neil and Jimmy, who were laughing like hyenas, but Michelle placed her hand on mine.

'Don't, Jax. It's not worth it.'

I sat down again.

'So what plans do we have? Give up?' said Jasper, trying to sound inspirational. 'Did Captain Scott of the Antarctic give up? Or Douglas Bader in the Battle of Britain?'

We all looked at each other, confused and a little worried.

'Didn't Captain Scott die trying to get to the South Pole?' said Charlie.

'Yes, and I'm pretty sure Douglas Bader lost both his legs,' said Michelle.

'Well, uh, yes. But they didn't give up, that's the point.'

'You're treating it like it's a military operation, Jasper,' said Michelle. 'We're a bunch of eleven-year-olds. What can we possibly do?'

Jasper seemed to take this as a challenge to his intellect and he sat quietly for a few moments, his chin resting on his fingertips, which were pressed together as if in quiet prayer.

'What's above the head's office?' he asked.

'Nothing,' said Charlie. 'It's a single-storey building. There's nothing but a flat roof and a load of pigeon poo.'

'Then we go up there and work our way in from the outside. We drill though the roof and drop down from upon high, with safety harnesses and torches! Come on, gang, what do you say?'

'I say you've been watching too many films,' I said. 'Why don't we just go to Mr Kirrin and tell him what's happening?'

'He'd never believe us,' said Jasper. 'He hasn't even reported the trophy missing and besides, I think he's still angry with me from the time I rewired all the automatic doors in the school so that they closed as you walked towards them.'

Jasper finally looked defeated, which was something I'd never seen before. He was the life and soul of the Codebusters and seeing him look so sad and disheartened seemed to spur me on.

'But we can't give up now! Like you said, we're the smartest guys in the room and we can achieve anything we want.'

'Ow!' A particularly hard chip hit Michelle square in the back of the head.

'And we can start by defending ourselves,' I said. I was angry now and strangely motivated. 'Charlie, what drink have you got today?'

'Blackcurrant juice, why?'

'Can I borrow the bottle?'

He nodded and rooted around in his bag, bringing out a jumbo bottle of purple juice. It looked as though it consisted of half a bottle of squash diluted with only a tiny bit of water – Charlie liked his drinks sweet.

'Okay, quiz time – what happens when fast moving air passes over a straw?' I asked.

Jasper and Michelle looked confused.

'Um...that's Bernoulli's Principle. It creates an area of low air pressure,' said Jasper.

'It would cause any liquid to rise up the straw. It's called the Venturi effect,' said Michelle. 'Why?'

I grabbed two straws off the table and put one in the bottle, plunging it deep into the purple liquid. What I was about to do was mad, possibly dangerous, but I couldn't see any other way. Besides, it'd be fun.

I placed the other straw horizontally next to the top of the vertical straw, keeping them straight with my finger and thumb. The straws were at a perfect right angle to each other.

'Er... what are you doing?' said Michelle, frowning at me like I'd lost the plot.

'Getting our own back and killing two birds with one stone.'

I glanced at the table behind us, where Neil and Jimmy sat.

'Careful, mate. If you blow into that, it'll spray all over... oh, right!' Charlie smiled as he realised what I was up to.

'What? What's he doing?' said Jasper, panicking as I rose from the table. 'The man's a loose cannon! What's he doing?'

I walked slowly over to Neil and Jimmy's table. They hadn't noticed, but a few people had clocked me and stared in my direction.

'What do you want, *Zero*?' said Jimmy, seeing me.

'You seem to be throwing chips at my friend.'

'So?' said Neil.

'So I thought you might want a drink to go with them.' I aimed the bottle at the two of them and closed my mouth around the horizontal straw. I blew as hard as my lungs would allow.

PFFFFT!

The thick blackcurrant squash travelled up the straw and sprayed in a fine mist all over the table, covering Neil and Jimmy in a sticky purple goo. The laughs were directed at them now, as the entire hall looked round to see what had caused the commotion. Neil and Jimmy were amazed. They'd never had anyone stand up to them before, let alone had an entire school laughing at them.

I smiled and looked over to my table, where Charlie was crying with laughter, Jasper was open-mouthed with shock and Michelle just smiled. She caught my eye and mouthed a simple 'thank you'. I smiled back.

It was only seconds before one of the lunch-duty teachers grabbed me by the shoulder and escorted me out of the hall, to a great cheer from the rest of the school.

'That was a stupid thing to do,' said the teacher.

'Yes, it probably was,' I admitted. 'Where are we going?'

'Where do you think?' he said. 'To see Mr Kirrin.'

'Ah. Good.'

I whipped out my phone and quickly thumbed a text to Michelle using the OSCAR app:

Off to head's office. Now it's your turn – need 5 mins distraction.

I hit 'send' and allowed myself a moment to grin.

'All part of the plan.'

Chapter Ten

Mr Kirrin wasn't impressed at having his lunch interrupted to deal with a student. He still had lasagne around his mouth when he arrived and told me to go into his office. I took a brief look around. Typical office stuff really. Photos of himself in the local newspaper pinned to a board, framed letters from proud parents and amusing cartoons of teachers doing daft things were Blu-tacked to the wall. I didn't see anything that could be a clue, but then it probably wasn't obvious, otherwise Mr Kirrin might have suspected something himself. He sat down opposite me, placing a mug of coffee on the desk.

'You're new, aren't you? Jackson, is it?'

'I prefer Jax, sir.'

'Yes, well, hmm,' he tutted. 'I prefer to eat my lunch in peace, but we can't all have what we want, can we, *Jackson*?'

'No, sir.'

He absent-mindedly pressed a button on his laptop. I sat silently, eager to keep the meeting going until the rest of the Codebusters came up with a distraction. It would have to be a good one to get Mr Kirrin out of his office long enough for me to find the clue. I had no idea what they'd come up with, but was confident they'd do it.

'What are we here for?' he said.

'Oh, general unruly behaviour,' I said vaguely.

'What *precisely*?'

I tried to string the story of the chip-throwing and the home-made blackcurrant air gun for as long as possible, so I made up some bits as well.

'... I just wanted to defend myself and my friends, so I armed myself, much like the home guard did in the Second World War. I like history, do you, sir? It's one of my favourite subjects. Ooh, is that a teaching award?'

I was *really* waffling now, my eyes darting about, half looking at the ceiling for clues, half looking out of the window for Michelle's distraction. Mr Kirrin must have thought I was really weird.

I think he might have scribbled down something like that on my permanent file.

'So,' he said, interrupting my stream of nonsense, 'your friends were being bullied, so you sprayed two boys with juice?'

'That's the long and the short of it, sir, yes.'

He sighed.

'That's very admirable, Jackson, but that's not the way things are done here at Bletchley Grange. We're a forward-thinking school and I can't have shenanigans like this going on when we've such a high-profile launch of our "Green Initiative" coming up. There are going to be people from the press around, waiting to see our new eco-boiler and they'll be looking at the school in general, including behaviour.'

He went on for a bit about being an ambassador for the school and improving standards. Just when I thought he was going to let me go, he reached for the phone.

'Of course, I'll have to call your mother.' What? No! I nearly shouted. I hadn't thought about that. This was serious. Where was Michelle with the distraction?

'Can't I just have a detention? I've learned my lesson, honestly, sir. I'll be a model student from now on, you won't hear a peep out of me.'

'I'm afraid not. This sort of thing would usually call for –'

He was interrupted by a frantic knocking on the door. It was the school secretary.

'Can't it wait, Maureen?' said Mr Kirrin.

'No, sir!' she said in a panic. 'At the front gate, sir. It's... it's... OFSTED!'

A look of total horror came over Mr Kirrin's face. I smiled. If this was Michelle's distraction, she couldn't have thought of a more perfect one. It was the thing that all head teachers fear the most.

'School inspectors? Now?' he said, his voice wavering. He rose and gathered some papers before charging out. He stopped, turned round, remembering I was there, and popped his head back in the door.

'You! Stay!'

'I'm not going anywhere, sir!' I smiled.

I waited until he was gone and got up to look around the room again. I had to be quick, as he'd soon realise that the inspection was a hoax.

What had the riddle said? *Find a clue above your head.* I checked all the frames on the wall, just in case there was a clue tucked behind them or written on the back (a tip I had picked up from Grandad's old war books), but I had no luck. I looked directly up and stared at the ceiling. It was one of those suspended ceilings, with polystyrene tiles that sat on a metal grid that hung from the roof above. I checked the door again to make sure the secretary's office outside was empty. It was, everyone having left in a hurry to warn the rest of the teachers.

I climbed carefully on to the desk, thinking how to explain myself to Mr Kirrin if he suddenly walked in on me at that moment. I reached up and lifted the ceiling tile, sliding it out of the way. I could just see the edge of a rolled-up piece of paper.

Pulling on it, I dislodged a load of dust and dirt, which came tumbling down on me and the desk. I coughed like an old man, and sneezed, putting the ceiling tile back and jumping down, the piece of paper in my hand. I frantically shook off what dust I could, and used my hands to scrape the dirt off the desk. Just then I heard the door go outside, and the chattering of Maureen, the secretary.

'Sorry about that, Mr Kirrin, but I had no reason to doubt them. That Michelle's such a good girl. She never usually fibs.'

I panicked, my hands full of dust and grime, so I put the contents into Mr Kirrin's coffee mug, praying he wouldn't be thirsty when he came back. Stuffing the clue into my pocket, I sat back down on my chair just as he opened the door.

'False alarm,' he said, sounding relieved. 'Somebody's idea of a joke, no doubt.' He sat back down, obviously shattered from running the length of the school to the gates and finding that Michelle, Charlie and Jasper had made it all up.

'All right, Jackson, be off with you,' he said.

'Sir?'

'You'll have a detention, during which you can compose a written apology to your victims.'

I smiled. 'You're not calling my mum?'

'You're lucky. I haven't got the energy any more. Now go on, get out.'

I rose eagerly, desperate to escape. I closed the door behind me as Mr Kirrin raised his coffee mug to his lips, after which I heard the unmistakable sound of dusty coffee being spat across a room.

I scarpered.

Back in the corridor, I congratulated myself on a good plan, well executed. I fished the little scroll out of my pocket and looked at the next clue:

> *You've found a clue!*
> *Now find one more,*
> *Where HCl*
> *Meets H_2SO_4*

I punched the air in victory and ran off down the corridor.

Chapter Eleven

This was just *too* easy! I was no genius and if the truth be told, pretty awful at science, but I knew from my first few chemistry lessons at my old school that HCl and H_2SO_4 were chemical symbols. Okay, I didn't know *what* they stood for, but it didn't matter. All I had to do was find them and even *I* could work out that I needed to get to a chemistry lab.

My phone beeped and up popped a message on the secure OSCAR app. It was a video of Jasper, his hair filling the screen.

'Mr Hilbert! Contact me *immediately* on this secure frequency. That is an order!'

I'm not sure why I did it, but I deleted the message and didn't call him. I was doing all right on my own, and if I'm honest, I felt like showing off. Who did Jasper think he was to order me around anyway? He might *think* we were in the army, but he wasn't *my* commanding officer.

I passed a few people who patted me on the back for dealing with Neil and Jimmy and a few who pretended to be scared of me, saying I was some weirdo who might attack them at any minute with a bottle of squash. Actually, they may not have been *pretending* to be scared...

I made my way to the old chemistry lab, our HQ – it seemed the obvious place to start looking. No one was there and I thought how cool it would be to say that I had found the clue in the head's office, solved it, and then found the next one, all by the time I saw Jasper, Michelle and Charlie again.

Where would the clue be though? Somewhere hidden, of course. We'd have noticed it if it was in plain sight. I looked under benches, up at the old blackboard, even behind a poster of the periodic table.

My phone beeped again. A text from Michelle this time:

Where are you? Did you get expelled?
Watch out – Neil & Jimmy are after you ;-)

I laughed, but held off texting back as I wanted to let her know I'd found the next clue.

Just then, I saw a door that I hadn't noticed before on the far wall. I went over and took a closer look. It was a store cupboard, with notices on the front saying 'No Entry', 'Hazardous Materials' and a big one that said 'STAFF USE ONLY'. Inside, it was small but just deep enough for a person to fit. I used the light from my phone to look at the jars and bottles on the shelves, all chemicals, acids and alkalis. The clue *must* be in here, I thought, and peered in further.

Just then I felt a sharp jab in the small of my back and I staggered forward into the cupboard. I dropped my phone as I put my hands out to stop myself from crashing into the shelves of bottles.

SLAM! the door went behind me and I was plunged into darkness. I turned just in time to hear the click of a key being turned, locking me in.

'Oi!' I yelled, thumping on the door in panic. I yelled harder, hoping it was just another student playing a prank. Deep in my heart, though, I knew this was no joke. I paused for breath and heard a low, muffled laugh outside.

Elgar. It had to be.

'I know you're out there,' I shouted. 'And we'll defeat you in the end, so you may as well let me out right now!'

The laughter continued but became distant as the footsteps walked slowly out of the lab, leaving me stuck in the cupboard like a right lemon.

I've never been scared of small spaces, but then again I've never been locked in a cupboard of hazardous chemicals by an unknown prankster before, and it's amazing how quickly it starts to feel like you're in a coffin. I thumped and yelled some more, panicking slightly as claustrophobia set in.

I reached for my phone to call one of the Codebusters, but remembered that I'd dropped it. I knelt down in the darkness of the cupboard and felt around the floor. There was no sign of it. I heard a buzz as it vibrated, signalling a message, so I searched quickly for the light it produced as the screen lit up. A tiny shimmer came from the gap below the door. I could just about crouch in the tiny space, so I got down and pressed my face to the floor. There it was, my phone, glowing away... on the other side of the door.

I grunted in annoyance. Typical! An idea came to me and I felt around for something, anything, to hook the phone through the gap. Maybe a ruler or a pen or something, but I couldn't find anything in the dark of the cupboard. I removed my belt (thanks for buying trousers that were too big for me, Mum!) and slipped it under the door. After a few minutes of trying, I had managed to knock the phone closer to the door. With a final flick, I brought it closer to me, but with a *thunk!* it hit the door, too thick to slide though the gap.

I thumped the door in frustration. I stood and pulled my arm back to see if I could give it a push outwards, maybe force it open. As I did so, my arm hit a shelf full of bottles, which rolled off and shattered as they hit the floor.

'Oh, bum,' I said, but the words going through my head were a lot worse. I was worried about the broken glass and the trouble I might get into with a teacher when they found me (or maybe *if* they found me?). It turned out that I had a lot more to worry about. The chemicals I had spilled started to mix together on the floor and soon I could smell an awful, toxic stench. I began to cough and my eyes started to water from the smell being produced. I had managed to smash chemicals that would combine to produce a poisonous gas! Not only that, but I had purposefully not told anyone where I was going and no one was looking for me.

I was *well* doomed.

Chapter Twelve

I hammered on the door like a maniac, but I could feel myself getting dizzy from the fumes. I eventually gave up and leant back on the door. I think I may have passed out for a few seconds because the next thing I remember was stumbling back and falling to the floor as the door opened behind me. I looked up from the ground and saw Charlie, Michelle and Jasper standing over me. Actually, that's not quite true – I saw two of each of them above me, my mind still recovering from the toxic gases.

'What are you playing at?' said Charlie. 'I've been trying to phone you.'

Jasper picked my phone up off the floor.

'It seems Mr Hilbert wasn't able to talk. Turn those fans on will you, Mr Babbage? Before we all suffocate.'

Charlie flicked a switch on the wall and a couple of extractor fans whirred into life, sucking the harmful gases out of the room. I breathed deeply, enjoying every lungful of clean air, and my head began to clear.

'Really, what on earth did you think you were doing, Mr Hilbert?'

'I wanted –' I interrupted myself by coughing – 'I wanted to solve the clue on my own.' I passed them the original scroll of paper with the riddle on it. Michelle nodded.

'I can see why it led you here. Did you find the next clue?'

I shook my head and told them how I'd been locked in the cupboard by Elgar and nearly gassed myself to death.

'Is this it?' said Charlie. There was a piece of notepaper lying on the floor just outside the cupboard. He picked it up and handed it to Jasper, who frowned and nodded.

'I think your powers of observation need honing, Mr Hilbert. The clue was in plain sight all along.'

'It wasn't there when I opened the cupboard!' I said. I was hurt that my detecting skills were being called into question. 'It must have been taped to the inside of the door and it fell off when Elgar pushed me inside!"

'Why would Elgar lead you here and then trap you?' said Jasper.

'I don't know! Why would he steal a stupid maths trophy? Have you ever asked yourself that?'

'Jax!' Michelle looked shocked at my outburst.

'Come on! If our prankster's anything like the Professor says, why nick a kid's silly cup? It's not as if it's worth anything!'

I knew I was well out of line. I was angry at having been locked up and I was tired after shouting for help. I was taking it out on my friends, but the truth was that I was angry with myself. Charlie placed a hand on my shoulder.

'Calm down, mate. You've been through a lot.'

I shrugged him away and sulked off to the corner of the room.

'He stole the trophy to send a message. He must know who the Codebusters are and what we do,' said Jasper, quite calmly. He adjusted his glasses, the only sign that I had upset him. 'He knows what the trophy means to Michelle and myself.'

'You shouldn't go off on your own like that, Jax. We're a team for a reason you know,' said

Michelle. Everyone was being very calm and kind, considering how I was behaving.

'Can I see the code?' I said, coming over to join them again. 'I *did* almost sacrifice a lung for it.'

Jasper laid the piece of paper on a desk.

5, 37, 2, 23, 41 / 97, 47, 73, 61 / 53, 61, 23, 101, 11
/ 23, 43 / 59 / 3, 37, 47, 5, 31

I stared at the problem for a while.

'Sorry, guys, I've got nothing,' I said. 'I'm too tired and my brain's frazzled from that gas.' I picked up my bag and walked out of the door. I was halfway down the corridor when I heard Michelle's light footsteps run up behind me.

'Jax! You forgot your phone,' she said, handing it to me.

'Thanks,' I said. 'Sorry I was really horrible to you all just now.'

'Don't worry,' she smiled. 'I think Jasper wants you court-marshalled though.'

'He doesn't like me much does he?'

'In his words? *The man's a loose cannon!*' She did a surprisingly good impression of Jasper.

'Thanks for before, with Neil and Jimmy. No one's ever stood up for me like that.'

I found myself blushing.

'Yeah, well, I did it for the group really.' Why did I say that? Michelle thought I had done something gallant and gentlemanly, and then I go and tell her it was all part of the job. 'It was the perfect way to get into Mr Kirrin's office, so I –' Shut *up*, Jax!

'No, it's fine, I understand.' Michelle turned away, a slightly crushed look on her face. I had hurt her feelings, practically said she alone wasn't worth the detention, and I didn't know how to take it back.

'I didn't mean –'

But she was gone.

Chapter Thirteen

I sauntered home that evening, not wanting to hang out at school and not wanting to get back and explain my bad mood to Mum. I kicked a stone as I walked along the street. I had taken a meandering route and was a little bit lost. I would be able to retrace my steps when I wanted to go home, but for now I was happy enough to potter along, left to my own thoughts.

I had been having a long think about the Codebusters and thought it was time I should leave. I didn't like how dangerous it was getting. It had started out as a chance to do some puzzles with my mates, but being locked in a cupboard and nearly being poisoned by toxic gases wasn't really my idea of fun. I had lost my enthusiasm for it all and had convinced myself that I was going to quit the next day after school.

Part of me knew that I was disheartened because of Elgar. I couldn't see how we could beat him. He was fast, clever, and locking me in that cupboard had proved how dangerous he could be. The latest clue seemed hard too. I had spent the afternoon trying to puzzle it out, but I couldn't make any sense of it at all. The slashes in between the numbers may indicate spaces, which meant that each set of numbers was a word, and each number was a letter. But no one could work it out, not even OSCAR the supercomputer.

Just then I saw Jasper at the end of the street. It was a long road and it was getting dark, but it was definitely him – how many other kids have a huge mass of curly hair and a briefcase? I wouldn't have expected to see him there. The neighbourhood I was walking through was a bit rough and rundown. I had always imagined Jasper's house to be... actually, I hadn't imagined Jasper's house at all. I think I thought he lived in a giant silver computer lab or something, connecting his brain to a bunch of machines like a scientist in a bad black-and-white movie. I certainly hadn't expected him to live in one of the places I was near now – dirty terraced houses, with broken-down cars and rubbish in their front gardens. He hadn't seen me, but I decided that I would go and tell him that I was leaving the Codebusters right now. It would get it over with and then I wouldn't have to face Michelle and Charlie the next day. I jogged up behind him.

'Jasper!'

He turned and flinched, holding up his briefcase in front of him like a shield.

'Calm down. It's me,' I said and he lowered the case. He seemed surprised and a bit flustered.

'Mr Hilbert? W-what on earth?' he stammered.

'I was just passing and I needed to talk to you. I –'

At that moment, the door opened to the house we were in front of and a large Jamaican woman stepped out.

'Jasper! You gonna stand there all day? Your dinner's going on the table this second!' She saw me and smiled a big warm smile. 'Who's this? You gotta friend?' She sounded genuinely surprised.

'Hardly, Mother,' said Jasper. 'A school acquaintance perhaps.'

My manners kicked in and I went to shake her hand.

'I'm Jackson, Mrs Newton. Pleased to meet you. Call me Jax.'

'I'll do no such thing! Such a fine name, why do you go shortening it? Come on in, we've got plenty of food to go round!'

Jasper obviously didn't want me to and I tried to leave, but I was already getting pulled through the door into the house. As it happened, Mum was working late, so she wouldn't be home for ages. I fired off a text to tell her not to buy fish and chips for me on the way home and was plonked down on a seat at a large table opposite Jasper. I was surrounded by the rest of the Newtons. Jasper was from a big family, the middle child of five. There was Eddy, the eldest, then Julie, with long braided hair and a school uniform (she obviously went to a different school to us). Two younger children sat at the end of the table, Samuel and Anthony, who squabbled and squirmed until Mrs Newton's giant hands forced them into their seats. They said grace and dived into the food, which sat in the middle of the table in mounds. It was real home cooking, the best I'd ever tasted, and enough to feed an army! Around the table, brothers and sisters talked over each other, argued, laughed and sang. I loved it. At home it was usually just me and Mum, sat in front of the telly with trays on our laps, but this mealtime was electric. Strangely though, Jasper seemed to get lost in the hubbub. The big powerful personality I was used to seeing shrank smaller and smaller around the rest of his family until he looked like... well, like a quiet eleven-year-old boy, not the gawky sergeant major I was used to seeing at school.

Occasionally, he glanced up to meet my eye, and his look was filled with embarrassment. I don't think his family embarrassed him, it was more the way he acted around them. When our bellies were full to bursting and we'd been offered second helpings, we were released from the table. I offered to help with the dishes (mums love it when you do that, and they hardly ever take up the offer), but we were shooed away.

'Get off with you!' she grinned. 'Jasper will take you up to his room. So glad you could come, Jackson. Jasper hardly ever brings friends home.'

'*Mother!*' said Jasper.

He reluctantly led me up the stairs. We passed a picture on the wall, a framed photo of a smart man in an army uniform. We went to his bedroom, a

tiny box room only just big enough to fit a single bed and a small desk with his laptop on it. The computer was a bit of a home-made job, bound together with pieces of soldered metal and black gaffer tape, with a large webcam on the top.

'I'm sorry you had to see that, Mr Hilbert.'

'What do you mean?' I smiled. 'Your family's ace!'

'Hmm,' he said, neither agreeing nor disagreeing. 'You had something to report?'

I paused. I didn't want to tell him I was leaving. Not yet.

'That man in the photo. Is that your dad?' I asked. Jasper nodded. 'He's a captain in the army? That's kind of cool. Is he away much?'

Jasper folded his arms and looked down at the carpet.

'He's on his second consecutive tour of duty. He hasn't been home for fifteen months.'

I quickly calculated the time in my head. Mr Newton – *Captain* Newton – would have left just before Jasper started at Bletchley Grange, and before he started the Codebusters with Professor Turing.

'Does he know about the Codebusters? Or your maths trophy?'

Jasper was silent. I knew he didn't want me to be there. I had insulted him at school and barged into his home. He looked uncomfortable.

'I was going to tell him, but...'

Suddenly everything fell into place. How could I have been so stupid? I had seen how Jasper had got lost in the mass of kids at the dinner table. It must be hard to be noticed in such a big family.

'You were going to video call him and show him the trophy, weren't you? To surprise him?'

I felt completely rotten. I had called the trophy worthless, but it meant so much more to Jasper than he was letting on. It had been his chance to show his dad what he was good at, and to connect with him.

'You had something to report?' he repeated, ignoring my question. But I couldn't tell him I was leaving now, could I? Tell him I was giving up, and that I wouldn't even try to help him find his trophy?

'I...' My phone beeped, interrupting me. I looked at it, and flinched as I saw a message on the screen. I showed Jasper:

TICK-TOCK, GOES THE CLOCK,
YOU CAN SEARCH, BUT YOU
WON'T SEE!

YOU'RE GETTING HOT, BUT NOT A LOT, THE CODEBUSTERS CAN'T CATCH ME!

'The cheek!' exclaimed Jasper. 'What did you want to say, Mr Hilbert? If that's it then I'd ask you to leave me in peace to work out this wretched clue!'

I pocketed my phone and stood up straight.

'I just wanted to apologise for my behaviour earlier. I disobeyed a direct order and it won't happen again –' I paused and added for good measure – 'sir!'

Jasper seemed pleased at my formal, army-style tone of voice. Now I knew how much the trophy meant to him, I was going to do everything I could to help him get it back. And if I had to treat him like a sergeant major while we did, then that was fine with me.

'Very well, Mr Hilbert. Apology accepted. Stand down.'

I shook his hand and left him to his computer. Then I walked home, trying to puzzle out how on earth I was going to crack that code.

Chapter Fourteen

I sat in maths wrapped up in my coat due to the chilly temperature. The autumn weather had taken a real turn and everyone was in their jumpers and scarves, moaning about the cold. I watched Miss Almond write up problems on the board, but I didn't even try to solve them. My mind was constantly going over the clue and I couldn't think about anything else.

'And who can remember what the magic ingredient in this equation is? Anyone?' said Miss Almond. Thirty blank faces looked back at her. 'Jax?' She looked at me desperately. The answer was locked away somewhere in my brain, but I couldn't raise the enthusiasm to work it out. Even my love of maths had gone. I shrugged.

'Sorry, miss.'

She sighed and passed the question on to Michelle, who was sitting a few rows behind me.

'Pi, miss,' she said. 'Three point one four.'

I glanced back at her. She saw me and quickly looked away. I had smoothed things over with Jasper, but my friendship with Michelle had gone down the toilet. One minute I'm her hero, standing up for her against the bullies. The next I'm gabbling away, saying I didn't do it for her after all. And the *real* kicker about everything is that no matter how much I try to blame Elgar, the only person I've really got to blame is myself. *I* chose to join the Codebusters, *I* found the first note from Elgar, *I* went off on my own, and *I* knocked over the bottles of chemicals in the cupboard. However miserable I was, it was all down to me.

'Greetings, Bletchley Grange!' The screen at the front of the class had buzzed into life. Mr Kirrin's head appeared and there was something strange about him. He was *smiling*. 'Forgive me for interrupting your lessons, but I have a special announcement. The new eco-boiler that has been installed underneath Q Block will be turned on this afternoon! The cold weather has brought forward our opening ceremony and the mayor will be unveiling the new heating system very soon. We have collected enough waste to burn throughout the winter and our state-of-the-art system can reach temperatures of nine hundred degrees centigrade! As you can tell, I'm very excited. Bletchley Grange will become an "Eco School" very soon and you won't need to wear all those coats and scarves. Good day!'

The class cheered at the idea of being able to take off their layers and Miss Almond struggled to get their attention back to the problems on the board.

'Settle down now!' she shouted over the din. 'As I was saying, this is a *prime* example of –'

CLANG! Something in my head fell into place. That was it! The key to the last clue!

Somehow Elgar knew all about the Codebusters, so maybe he would create a code based around the thing that had got me into the gang in the first place – *prime numbers*. I quickly scribbled down the alphabet on my exercise book. I then started to write down all the prime numbers above the letters – 2, 3, 5, 7, and so on. It was tricky, as Miss Almond was at the front of the class shouting out numbers to her own separate problems and confusing me. I was also shaking with excitement and eager not to mess it up. Halfway through I panicked and forgot the entire sequence.

Miss Almond clapped her hands to get the attention of the class.

'I want you to work on the next problem in pairs, so mix yourselves up.'

Yes! I had no idea what she was talking about, but I shot to my feet. I charged over to Michelle, almost barging another girl out of the way.

'What do you want?' said Michelle.

'Michelle, I know you're upset with me, but I only want to be your friend. The group means a lot to me and I think I've cracked the code. I just need your help.'

She frowned.

'You're not going to go off on your own?'

I shook my head.

'Not after last time.'

She looked at me, thinking over whether to give me another chance.

'Sit down,' she ordered. I plonked myself down next to her and we worked on cracking the code. Michelle was much quicker and calmer than me and soon we had pieced together the key. I connected to OSCAR on my phone, where

Jasper had copied the clue. We wrote the original clue down underneath our key.

2	3	5	7	11	13	17	19	23	29	31	37	41
A	B	C	D	E	F	G	H	I	J	K	L	M
43	47	53	59	61	67	71	73	79	83	89	97	101
N	O	P	Q	R	S	T	U	V	W	X	Y	Z

5, 37, 2, 23, 41 / 97, 47, 73, 61 / 53, 61, 23,
101, 11
/ 23, 43 / '59' / 3, 37, 47, 5, 31

We then matched each number to its letter, uncovering what the clue said. When it was finished, we stared at the message for a few seconds.

'What do you think?'

'I think we'd better hurry.'

Chapter Fifteen

Michelle and I leapt up, grabbing our bags and books, and making a dash for the door. Miss Almond stepped in front of us, her arms crossed.

'Jax? Michelle? Where do you think you're going?'

'Please, Miss, it's an emergency,' I said.

'We have to act *now*, Miss!' said Michelle, a touch dramatically. As we all know, pleading never works with teachers. It just makes them dig their heels in even further.

'Have you solved the problem on the board?'

'Er... no,' I admitted. 'We were working on an independent project.'

'My two best mathematicians, stuck on a problem? I never thought I'd see the day.' She sighed.

'Please, Miss! You know we can do it!'

'Go on, then,' Miss Almond said, calling our bluff. We both stared at the board. The problem was probably quite simple, but with the excitement, panic and terror running through us, neither of us could concentrate on the numbers. I gave a pathetic shrug.

'Sorry, guys,' said Miss Almond. 'You'll have to save the world another day. Take a seat.'

We sloped back to our desks and waited until the end of the lesson. I sprang up when the bell finally went, but Miss Almond delighted in keeping us in our seats for a minute or so longer while she explained the homework.

Finally Michelle and I were able to bolt out of the door and I tapped my phone until the friendly blue OSCAR screen lit up. I pressed the communications button and keyed in Jasper's and Charlie's contacts. Within seconds, their faces appeared on the screen, a video conference taking place as we walked down the corridor.

'Team leader to troops, receiving you loud and clear, over,' barked Jasper.

'Yo!' said Charlie.

'We figured out the clue,' said Michelle. 'It used prime numbers instead of letters.'

'Of course!' said Jasper. 'And the message?'

'CLAIM YOUR PRIZE IN Q BLOCK,' I said, reading from the scrap of paper.

'Q Block? Isn't that where the new eco-boiler is?' said Charlie.

'Yes, and it's due to be turned on any second! It would be just like Elgar to wedge the trophy in the boiler. We need to –' I stopped as I noticed something in the background of Charlie and Jasper's pictures on the screen. It was the back of my head.

I turned to face them. Somehow we had ended up in the same corridor.

'We need to stop the opening ceremony until we can get to the boiler and fish out the trophy.'

'They can't start without the mayor,' said Charlie. 'I'll block the front gate.'

'How?'

He produced a bike lock from his bag. It had a four-number combination lock.

'It'll take them ages to crack this code!' he said, smiling devilishly.

'I'll create a distraction,' said Jasper. 'The whole heating system has electronic sensors that feed back to the school's main computer. I'll get OSCAR to hack into the system. They won't start up the boiler if they think there's a problem with the pipes.'

I marvelled at how well our little group seemed to be doing under pressure.

'Jax and I will head over to Q Block. We'll see if we can get the trophy before they turn it on,' said Michelle.

'You'd better hurry,' said Jasper, pushing up his glasses. 'The trophy is made of sterling silver, which melts at eight hundred and ninety-three degrees centigrade. If the boiler reaches full temperature, the only thing we'll have to show for our efforts is a mass of molten metal.' He shuddered at the thought. 'Codebusters – good luck!'

Michelle and I jogged off towards Q Block. It was lunchtime, so there were quite a few people about. We left the main building and headed off in the right direction, across a playground, but –

'Jax! You and me have got unfinished business!' It was Jimmy, followed by Neil. We turned round to face them.

'I think you'll find that should be you and *I*,' said Michelle.

'Thanks, Michelle!' I whispered to her. 'I think he's angry enough with me without you correcting his grammar.'

'You think it was funny? Blasting me with juice like that?'

Now, what I was meant to say here was something along the lines of 'No, of course not. I'm so sorry, please forgive me'. Instead I burst out laughing as the image of Jimmy and Neil came back into my mind, dripping with blackcurrant squash. This wasn't the reaction they were expecting.

Michelle looked at me as though I was crazy.

'What? It *was* funny.'

'You're gonna pay!' shouted Neil. I turned to Michelle.

'Quick, you get to Q Block and get the trophy. I'll deal with these numbskulls.'

'You're going to fight them?' she said, looking worried.

'Don't be silly,' I said with a wink. 'I'm going to run for it.'

I dashed off in the opposite direction, sprinting for my life. Neil and Jimmy followed, as I hoped they would. I sped past the school buildings, zoomed through the playground and on to the open playing fields. The ground was slippery underfoot, but luckily I didn't fall.

Neil and Jimmy followed close behind, shouting insults and threats. They were fast, but I was faster, spurred on by the thought of avoiding a beating. I had lost my breath long ago but I only needed to run a hundred metres more for what I had planned.

I could hear their feet pounding on the mud as they chased me through a football match, ducking to keep out of the way of the ball. We approached the fence that marked the boundary of the school's land. I didn't know if they'd follow me this far, but I was counting on it. I stopped and waited for them to catch up while I got my breath back.

'You had enough?' said Neil when he got to me. Jimmy caught up, puffing away.

'No, I've got plenty of energy left,' I grinned. 'What do you want from me, fellas?'

'I want to hear you beg,' said Jimmy. 'Just like before!'

'What?' I said, confused.

'*I know you're out there,*' mimicked Neil with a whiney voice. '*And we'll defeat you in the end, so you may as well let me out right now!*' They both laughed cruelly.

'Wait, *you* locked me in that cupboard?'

'Why, made any other enemies recently?'

More than I'd like, I thought. But this meant Elgar had nothing to do with locking me in, and me nearly dying from toxic fumes. Maybe he *was* just the harmless prankster we'd first thought. I didn't have time to think about it further at that moment, however.

'You're gonna pray you never messed with us!' said Jimmy, now angrier than ever. I hoped my plan worked out, or I was in deep trouble. They both grabbed me by the arms and pinned me against the fence.

'I wouldn't do that if I were you,' I said, smiling.

Dan, Dave and Dom, the Bragg brothers, came up and leant against the fence to see what was going on. Neil and Jimmy's faces fell when they realised I'd lured them straight to the edge of the park next to school, the Braggs' turf.

'All right, Jax?' said Dan.

'Hi, boys. I know how much you like having friends to play football with, so I brought Neil and Jimmy here for a kickabout.'

'Cheers, mate!' said Dave.

Neil and Jimmy dropped me, and I dusted myself off, feeling very smug indeed. Dan and

Dom grabbed a boy each and lifted them over the fence like they were ragdolls.

'See you later, chaps!'

I headed back to the school, smiling as I heard the sound of the Braggs yelling their famous cry:

'BUNDLE!'

I caught up with Michelle a few minutes later outside Q Block.

'What's the matter? Why aren't you in there?'

'That's why.' She nodded to the building, which was rammed full of journalists, photographers and men in suits from the council. A dopey-looking boy from the year above us stood on the door, turning away kids who were trying to look in.

'Him? No problem!' I said, pushing Michelle forward. 'Come on.'

I walked up to the boy and nodded politely. As expected, he put his hand on my chest, halting me.

'No entry to students,' he mumbled.

'We're from the school paper,' I said. 'They're expecting us.'

The boy stared blankly at us for a second, then shook his head.

'Don't you know who this is?' I pointed to Michelle. 'She won the Young Journalist of the

Year competition last year. She's been published in all the major papers.' Michelle smiled sweetly at him.

'There isn't a school paper,' he said.

Oh, bum. I probably should have checked that out before jumping in with such a whopping lie.

'Not yet,' said Michelle. 'I'm writing for the first issue, and if you're not careful our first headline will be IDIOT SCUPPERS ECO LAUNCH, with a huge picture of your ugly face plastered across the front cover!'

Crikey, she was *really* getting into her role.

'All right, all right,' said the boy and let her past. As I went to go forward, he stopped me again. 'So if she's the writer, who're you?'

I flustered and panicked. I hadn't thought of that one. I quickly pulled my phone out.

'Photographer!'

I activated the camera on the phone and a flash went off in his face. He staggered back, blinded for a few seconds, and I ducked past him into the building. Pushing through the crowds of people, I heard my phone beep, so I answered it. It was Jasper.

'We're in!' I said, catching up with Michelle. 'How're you doing?'

'Not great,' said Jasper, disappointed. 'My plan has been compromised.'

'Meaning?'

'OSCAR couldn't hack into the heating system. It seems they have *very* sophisticated technology. Also, I *may* have turned on the fire sprinklers in Mr Kirrin's office by mistake.'

I sighed.

'Never mind. It doesn't look like the mayor is here yet. Maybe Charlie's plan worked.'

I hung up, but the phone rang straight away.

'My plan didn't work,' said Charlie down the line.

'What? Why?'

'They managed to crack the code on my bike lock.'

'How?' I thought for a few seconds. 'Charlie, what was the combination?'

'1234. Why?'

I sighed again.

'Anyway, I'm ringing because the mayor should be with you any second. Good luck!' He hung up just as the mayor entered the building through the main doors and the photographers started to snap away.

'We're on our own now,' I said to Michelle. 'It's up to you and me.'

I noticed the door to the basement, labelled with a brand-new sign that read: 'Boiler Room'. I grabbed Michelle by the hand and dashed through it. We crept down the steps, and turned to see the new eco-boiler. Shiny and huge, it filled the basement, with tubes and pipes coming out of it from all angles. Beside it stood hundreds of logs, made from recycled burnable rubbish that had been gathered from the school over the last year. The room was empty as Mr Kirrin, the mayor and everyone else were waiting upstairs to have their photos taken for the press. As far as I could tell, the recycled logs got put into a small door in the boiler, just like an old wood-burning stove.

'I can't see the trophy,' I said. 'Maybe we got it wrong.'

'I can see it,' said Michelle. She pointed to the small door where the fuel was loaded. Through a tiny glass window in the door, I could see the unmistakable glint of silver.

We ran down the rest of the stairs and rushed over to the eco-boiler. Smiling widely, I placed my hand on the handle.

'This way, your mayorship,' said Mr Kirrin's voice from the top of the stairs.

'They're coming!' hissed Michelle. 'Hide!'

She pulled me behind the pile of logs and we were able to peep through a gap to see what was happening. Mr Kirrin and the mayor walked over to the boiler, where a photographer took a few pics.

'Would you do us the honour of being the first to stoke the boiler and get our fire going?' said Mr Kirrin.

I nearly leapt up, but Michelle's hand forced me down again. The mayor began loading logs into the firebox, and we could see the trophy getting pushed further and further back, unnoticed by anyone except Michelle and me.

'The boiler works by pressure,' said Mr Kirrin. 'The heat is forced through these pipes out to the surrounding buildings, where it warms them using clean energy. All we need to do is press that big button and the eco-boiler will be activated!'

The mayor and Mr Kirrin smiled for the cameras and placed their hands on the big red button.

'Ready, everyone? Three, two, one –'

'NO!' I leapt up from my hiding place, but it was too late. The shock of me jumping out at them had made their hands slip, and they hit the button anyway.

'Jackson! What on earth?' exclaimed Mr Kirrin.

I ignored him, as I was concentrating on the boiler, which had started to clunk and hiss into action. The logs caught fire and the pressure began to build at an amazing rate. A dial on the side of the boiler began to climb and suddenly we all heard a clatter from inside.

'Should it be doing that?' asked the mayor.

'It's the trophy! The pressure has forced it through the pipes!' said Michelle, breaking her cover.

'Miss Chang?' Mr Kirrin was deeply confused now. The pipes coming out of the boiler began to bang and shake. The trophy was clanging through them, propelled by the pressure and heat, but there was no way of knowing which pipe it was in. They made a deafening noise in the tiny space.

'Would someone mind telling me what is going on?' shouted Mr Kirrin.

Suddenly, a pipe fell from the ceiling, breaking in two. Hot air began to rush from the pipe and seconds later the trophy clattered out of it, flying like a bullet towards the mayor, propelled by compressed air.

Without thinking, I put myself between the trophy and the mayor, diving though the air and

catching the trophy perfectly like a Premiership goalkeeper.

I landed on the ground, a hot but undamaged trophy in my hands and a rather stunned mayor and head teacher behind me. Michelle screamed with delight and applauded.

'We did it! We got the trophy! You were brilliant! Well caught! We should –'

'Ahem.' Mr Kirrin caught our attention. 'I don't know what just happened here, but I think you two should make yourselves scarce now.'

'Yes, sir!' We both got up and went to leave.

'And Jackson?' I stopped at the foot of the stairs. 'Good save. You should try out for the school football team.'

I smiled proudly, but looked to Michelle.

'I don't think so, sir. Maths is more my thing!'

Chapter Sixteen

All the Codebusters had gathered in Professor Turing's front room, the silver trophy was sitting on top of his piano. Michelle and I had returned from the eco-boiler room and hooked up with Jasper and Charlie. None of us could think about going home without celebrating, so after school we had gone to visit the Professor, who was very pleased to see us. He had welcomed us with a beaming smile and hearty handshakes, and a great spread of tea and cakes.

'May I propose a toast?' said the Professor, raising a teacup. 'To Jax, our hero.'

'To the Codebusters,' I corrected. 'A great team.'

'The Codebusters!' we all cheered and sipped from our steaming-hot cups.

'Although I could get used to the name "Hero"...' I mused.

'So you beat Elgar?' said the Professor. 'A tricky thing to do, let me tell you.'

'Yes, Professor, but we've yet to catch the bounder,' said Jasper. 'And I, for one, will not rest until we have.'

'I'm sure it's not the last we've heard of him,' said Michelle. 'He likes to show off, live on the wild side and put himself in the spotlight. We'll certainly be meeting up with him in the future, especially as we beat him this time. He'll be wanting revenge.'

'Actually, I may have overestimated how dangerous he can be,' I said. I told them how it was Neil and Jimmy who had locked me in the cupboard, not Elgar after all.

'I still don't trust him,' said Jasper. 'A thief is a thief.'

'Although the trophy never left the school grounds,' said the Professor. '*Technically* nothing was stolen. Curiouser and curiouser...'

Jasper drained his tea and leant forward, looking directly at me over his glasses.

'And what about you, Mr Hilbert? You were quite undecided about joining our little organisation. What do you make of us now?'

Everyone was staring at me. I swallowed my tea slowly.

'You lot? I think you're all mad, bad and dangerous to know.' Everyone laughed. 'But I'm very glad to be friends with you.'

'Awww!' said Charlie, pretending to cry. 'That's beautiful! Give us a cuddle!'

I pushed him away as he jokingly went to bear hug me.

'Of course, we need to swear you in,' said Jasper. Everyone groaned. 'What? This is an important part of being a Codebuster. Raise your right hand and repeat after me.'

For an easy life, I did as I was told. Jasper stood opposite me with his hand raised.

'I, Jackson Hilbert, do solemnly swear to uphold the values and secrets of the Codebusters, to protect its members and help others using my skills and knowledge.'

'Um... yeah. What you said,' I said, and slapped his hand in a high five.

'Looks like you're part of the team now, whether you like it or not,' said the Professor.

'That's fine by me,' I said, and sat down to have fun with my friends.

Codebusters Bootcamp

Attention recruits! This is sergeant major Jasper Newton speaking.

So you want to be in the Codebusters? Well, it's not that easy! First you'll have to crack these top-secret codes and puzzles. Good luck!

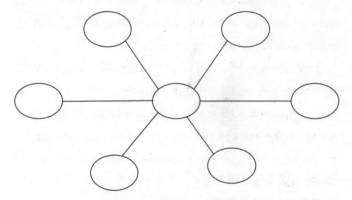

Put the numbers 1, 2, 3, 4, 5, 6 and 7 in the circles so that each straight line of three numbers adds up to the same total.

Use the code table on page 29 to decipher the following code:

LQNE YQU LPI JUP! SEE YQU PEXT TCDE!

Answers over the page...

How did you do?

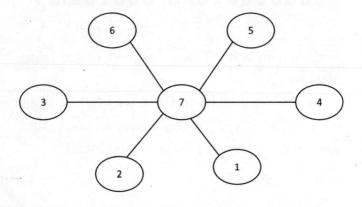

Each line now adds up to 14!

The code reads: HOPE YOU HAD FUN! SEE YOU NEXT TIME!

Why not use the codes in this book to send secret messages to all your friends!